Wheel F

Reluctantly I washed the sand off my feet, dried them with my handkerchief, put on my socks and shoes, and turned away from the sea to go back to the steps.

It was then that I saw it.

A weirdly formed piece of rock, that was my first impression.

I walked three steps nearer.

It was a trick of this deceiving light. That jet black shininess was some kind of reflection off the sea.

I walked forward another three slow steps.

A head. A body. Webbed feet. A dead seal washed up and abandoned by the receding tide.

I took two more steps towards it. Then I saw the half-human shape. Black rubber arms, aqualung equipment, two metal cylinders strapped to the back, the black-capped head on its side in the sand, the goggles smashed and broken.

The diver was lying on the beach, his flippered feet still trailing in the shallow water where the last big wave had just cast him up. He lay effortlessly, without struggle, as if he had been a long time dead.

For seconds I stood there frozen. When I did force myself forward, the sand glued my feet like steps in a nightmare. My breath gulped in my throat. Those few steps were like climbing a mountain. I thought even then: I'll wake up soon. The thing will have gone. Someone will come . . .

WHEEL FORTUNE

Karen Campbell

MAGNUM BOOKS
Methuen Paperbacks Ltd

A Magnum Book

WHEEL FORTUNE
ISBN 0 417 03450 4

First published in Great Britain 1973
by William Collins Sons & Co Ltd
Magnum edition published 1979

Magnum Books are published
by Methuen Paperbacks Ltd
11 New Fetter Lane, London EC4P 4EE

Made and printed in Great Britain
by Cox & Wyman Ltd,
London, Reading and Fakenham

For David

Thursday

It began with a kiss. A kiss by night on a deserted beach, my kiss to an unresponding stranger.

There had been nothing that morning to warn me. It was the twentieth of September – a Thursday. Just late enough for most of the St Edzell's holidaymakers to have returned home. Just early enough for few of the target beaches to be wired off. These days, one had to think of that. A sign of the times, as Mrs Luxford would say. In the last ten years, what I had come to regard as my little corner of Cornwall had grown some weird and alien industries – Porthdown, Goonhilly, Pendragon. Probably some more tucked away that no one was allowed to hear about. Though maybe not so alien, I corrected myself as I drove my Triumph Coupé smartly westward through easy traffic, considering Cornwall's formidable history.

It was a fine golden day and I drove fast. Had I left later or earlier, I would never have been involved. My life would have been quite different. So might the lives of other people.

I had been later than I intended leaving London. My director at the museum had wanted his newest acquisition, a Vladimir ikon, restored for an exhibition opening next week, and I had stayed up late the night before to do the finishing touches. I had packed hastily and skipped breakfast. But I didn't feel hungry, or as was later suggested a bit faint, and I didn't bother to stop for a cooked lunch. I knew Mrs Luxford would have a Cornish tea waiting, and be chewing her apron as she called it, with her eyes fixed on the old grandfather clock.

There was a savoury roast beef smell outside the comfortable façade of the Raleigh Hotel at Tavistock, and I hesitated. But I drove on through deserted streets and on to the new motorway cut through mountains of sugar-plum earth, through old villages, across stone bridges, dipping into boulder-strewn valleys where surprisingly swollen streams swept powerfully down – the speedometer needle touching ninety, foolishly making up time.

No warning sounded. Nothing caught at my imagination, except pleasure to be back home here again.

I skirted the edge of Bodmin Moor. It lay in a flood of amber light. Heather in full bell merged into its own purple mist. Waves of bracken fronds, uncrinkled yet by early frost, filled the hollows. Clumps of autumn beech and fretted birch stood with the breathing stillness of a Rowland Hilder landscape against a sky of bland and harmless blue.

Somewhere a bird of ill omen should have risen, one of Mr Luxford's dreaded hares should have leapt across the road. But there was nothing except the seagulls, and high on the hills ahead a comfortable brown line of Exmoor ponies.

Past Truro, the sun was in the south-west and full in my face. I had the Triumph's soft top down. The air was full of warm country sounds and smells. There were blackberries in the hedgerows and trails of shiny convolvulus fruit.

I slowed before the Falmouth roundabout. I was deep now in familiar countryside. I savoured it. From the top of every incline I glimpsed the almost blindingly colourless glitter of the sea, shadows of ships, crenellated headlands, saw the rock-strewn heath beyond the newly built bungalows. I passed the landmarks of the old mine engine-houses.

Wheal Manny Brown had grown more ivy in the last three years. Wheal Casper had lost the southern wall of its engine-house. There was a pile of sand and some white bricks by Wheal Caution as if someone like my father might be coming to open it up again.

With better luck, I hoped. My father is a mining engineer, and in my childhood, the reworking of the tin mines using modern methods had been the obsession of his life. We'd lived in St Edzell's, partly because my mother was an invalid, and partly because it's near Wheal Fortune. The mines were our connection with the Luxfords. He was an old man then – one of the last miners on the peninsula. He'd shared and encouraged my father's obsession, while Mrs Luxford had cleaned and cooked for us all, and muttered about time and money wasted and the sin of taking a child down the bowels of the earth for a treat instead of the paddling pool or the Fun Fair. Now my mother and Mr Luxford are dead, my father has married a Chilean lady with vast interests in some copper mine, and so, apart from Mrs Luxford, I have no real personal commitment to anyone.

Not that I have actually wanted any. Not total commitment, that is. I have always shrunk from the total commitment of marriage. I've always wanted to preserve something inside myself. The result, the psychiatrists would say, of a lonely childhood.

I leaned across and looked at myself in the driving mirror. I have a pale face with a pointed chin and high cheekbones. Grey eyes, that people say are my best feature, though they never tell one's worst. My hair is parted in the middle and at the museum I wear it in a French pleat, because it helps me to exude that aura of calm which persuades the director that I won't drop the Ming vase on the marble tiles. But that Thursday I let my hair whip out behind me in the Triumph's slipstream.

Past the turning to Gweek, I plunged into a winding high-hedged lane. It was the time for laden hay carts and turnip lorries, and I in my ignorance thought of no more dangers than that. I met a man on a bicycle driving a herd of cows up for milking. No other traffic.

I emerged from tunnels of green hedges on to what I think of as the last lap. Mrs Luxford now lives in an old coastguard cottage between Pendragon and St Edzell's. Five miles, no more. I began to think of tea.

Then I realized that this last lap was surprisingly good. Someone had taken most of the dangerous curves out of the road, cut back the hedges, widened it. The surface was freshly macadamed. I saw the reason when the Triumph purred round the last mild bend.

Royal Naval Air Station Pendragon had advanced like Birnam Wood. It had nibbled away at the countryside between it and the coast. Swallowed at least another mile of land.

Here the hedges had disappeared altogether. High steel mesh fenced the road. There were notices every few yards: *Government Property: Keep Out: No Admittance to Unauthorized Persons, Number Two Underwater Weapons Research Establishment.* The fence was interspersed with gates. There were guards at the gates. And beyond the fences indistinct with distance, long low buildings of concrete and glass, new hangars, silver as the insides of cigarette cartons, a massive control tower, a gaggle of helicopters on a huge hardstanding, and towering above a little clump of fir trees, three enormous dish-shaped radar scanners.

I lifted my foot off the accelerator and stared at those scanners irritably scouring the sky. They look so deceivingly blind. Like the blind beggar who is really the villain in disguise. I remember stopping and staring at them and thinking there is something frightening in a mechanism that can hear or see what we cannot hear or see. Though I didn't know then just *how* frightening.

And as I stared at them, one of the naval guards came out of his box, and pointed to another notice I hadn't seen: NO STOPPING ALLOWED.

And with words that I certainly could hear, ordered me to move on.

'Here's one that's not changed.' I heard Mrs Luxford's voice as I stepped out of the car. She stood framed in the front doorway of her cottage. And the cottage had changed.

It is made of blocks of Cornish granite, set squat and low on the headland, merging with it. The granite has the same veins of sparkling serpentine as the cliff, and the old stone roof had grown the same green lichen and even a few fronds of sea pink. Now the façade had been white Snowcemmed. There was a new gate and new telephone wires and a new concrete path leading up to the new front door.

There are no neighbours up this sandy lane, and no through traffic, so I left the car outside the gate. Just before I walked up the path I noticed in the way one notices inconsequential things that there were clear prints of fat tyres in the soft surface – a coal lorry perhaps, too heavy for a milk float.

'You haven't changed either,' I lied.

'I got meself three year more crop of wrinkles.' But it was more than that. There was an anxious shadow at the back of her button eyes. A look, had I not known her better, that I would have defined as guilty.

Then all anxiety and all shadows dissolved in her wide,

beaming smile. She spread her hands, brought them together to cup my face. She planted a quick kiss on my forehead, stood back as if to admire her handiwork.

In a thick emotional voice, '*Da yu genef agas gweles.*'

'And I'm glad to see you too.' I squeezed her hand.

'You're thinner than ever, though,' she said, swallowing her emotion. 'But that's not to be marvelled at. No one to cook proper meals for you.' Her voice was the same. Slow. Rich in its flattened vowels and rounded consonants. I used to think it was as if she slowly sucked melting butter.

'Your hair's been and darkened though, me dear.' She had said this to me last time. 'Colour of corn it used to be.'

I smiled. 'It's ripened.' I squeezed her hand. 'So have I, probably.'

It was then that I heard the helicopters coming right over us. Three of them, flying in line spread out like a Prince of Wales feather firework as they crossed the coast, teasing up the smooth surface of the sea with their slipstreams.

'It's like London Airport,' I said, looking up.

'They're from Pendragon. Blessed nuisance, but you get used to 'em, m'dear. It's only when they're exercising. Come along in. Set your bags down there, m'dear.' She pointed to the bottom of the narrow staircase. 'We won't go up till presently.'

I did as she told me.

She looked at my face expectantly waiting for me now to admire her nice new clothes and the cottage interior. Standing beside me like that, she was smaller than I remembered. Shrinking like an old picture. Sad. I rested my hand on her shoulder, and gave her a little hug.

'You're looking very smart,' I said. So she was. Her wispy mouse-grey hair was nicely cut and freshly set. There were two little blurs of lipstick where her cupid's bow once was, a dusting of powder over her purply cheeks. She wore a cream crêpe blouse with a frilly fichu, and with it, a large Victorian hair brooch.

'What about the house, m'dear? What do you think to this?'

'Super.' What else could I say? 'Very cosy, too.' I prodded the new brown carpet with my toe. The same carpet covered the living-room. There was a new floral-patterned rug in front of a new tile fireplace. Three small fat armchairs were arranged round it, a smart radiogram. A new clock ticked on the mantelpiece. There was a new gilt mirror above. Incongruously amongst it, uncomfortable in its new gilded frame, Mr Luxford peered out from under his miner's hard hat, surrounded by all his miner's impedimenta.

'You've certainly made some changes,' I said.

'Yes, well, things are a bit easier . . .' Mrs Luxford looked as if she might have said more and then decided that the moment was inopportune. 'I'll just go and mash up tea, m'dear. Everything's ready. Sit yourself down.'

'Shall I wash first?' I spread my hands. I felt sticky with the driving. 'I'll pop upstairs . . .'

'No, don't you bother yourself. Wash in the kitchen. I always do.'

Poor old dear, I thought. Those sturdy lisle-stockinged legs, not so able as they were to climb the stairs.

I followed her into the kitchen. There was vinyl substance on the floor, soft and cushiony to the feet, a new steel sink unit, a fridge, a washing-machine, and lots of little gadgets sticking out of the wall, all carefully hooded in little plastic covers. What Mrs Luxford had got, she'd had to work for and she wasn't going to neglect.

She opened a plastic bag and took out a piece of toilet soap, handed it to me, took out a clean towel from a drawer.

The view from the kitchen window was improved too. There were some late geraniums in the small flower-bed, gloxinia and nicotina. There was a new wooden fence and a new gate. Everything was very tidy. And more signs here too of her thrifty careful character – there were bolts at the kitchen windows and a hefty lock on the back door.

When I'd finished washing, Mrs Luxford wheeled the trolley through into the living-room. I followed. I sat opposite her in one of the fat armchairs. I faced the window. High up as we were, I could see to the far horizon. The sun itself was invisible behind long banks of cloud.

'Too bright a sun,' Mrs Luxford said, lifting the pot in its knitted teacosy. 'He'll rain, I shouldn't wonder, before the night's out.'

We discussed the weather. The wet August they'd had in the south-west, London's stifling nights, St Luke's little summer that we both hoped we were going to have. The swimming I was going to do, the walk on the beach I would have after tea. Chapel. The poor sermons Mrs Luxford heard these days, the new hymn tunes, the doleful singing. Mrs Luxford parted the folds of the linen-lined scone basket, released the delicious smell of her crusty home cooking. There was local butter on the trolley and a dish of Cornish cream, home-made strawberry jam and gingerbread.

'Help yourself, m'dear, and make a good tea.'

I buttered a scone and piled on the jam.

'I shall be fat before the fortnight's out.' Mrs Luxford looked as if she was going to say something again, and once again thought better of it.

'I was trying to work out, Livvy.' She handed me a china cup and saucer. 'How long is it since you lived in St Edzell's?'

'Nearly thirteen years. I was twelve when I left.'

'So you're pushing twenty-five, my dear.'

'The quarter-century.'

'You'll find St Edzell's very changed.'

'In what way?'

She didn't say. And predictably, as she had done since I was eighteen, 'Pretty girl like you. Did you never think of marrying and settling down?'

'I'm not quite past it yet, old friend,' I said, and smiled.

'Best early. I got married at sixteen. Mr Luxford was thirty-nine. Had a job, good job as a tut captain. *And* a cottage. That's the sort of man you want.'

I helped myself to another scone and said I would look out for such a paragon.

'Mind, you don't want to start a family. That's what's wrong with St Edzell's these old days.'

I raised my brows as I sipped my tea.

'Too many young 'uns, schoolgirls you might say, starting up a family because the Navy gives allowances.'

I chewed thoughtfully over her reasoning.

'Can't get into the Post Office for them of a Tuesday. Prams and push chairs.'

'Husbands work at Pendragon, I suppose.'

She nodded severely.

'I go every week and give a hand.'

'Not at Pendragon?'

'Oh no, it's very hush-hush there. Or *supposed to be*, you might say. I help at the welfare clinic. They asked for volunteers one morning after chapel. And I'd never had no little 'uns, so I thought I'd suit.'

'What d'you do?'

'Oh, what they call the unskilled work. Register the new 'uns. Weigh the babes. Give out the cod liver oil and orange juice. Cheer up the little mothers.'

'You'd be marvellous,' I said, and meant it.

'Most of 'em have never been before from their own mothers. They don't like Cornwall. They don't like their menfolk here and there of a night.'

'I take it,' I laughed, 'that I'm not to marry a naval chap.'

'Never!'

'I'd have a house.'

'And what houses you might say. Chicken houses. If someone sneezes they all hear it.'

'It's a wonder you haven't brought some of them here.'

'I do sometimes for tea.'

'I meant to *live*. I'm glad you kept my room . . .' She pursed her mouth. She looked more than ever like an anxious little monkey.

'Livvy . . . ?'

'Yes.'

'There's something I wanted to tell you. It's about your room.'

I said smiling, 'So long as you haven't given it to anyone else.'

She clasped her hands. 'But I have.'

I didn't believe her for a moment. I was surprised that I minded so much.

'So what? It doesn't matter. I've got a bed, have I?'

'Of course. The back room. To yourself. It's very nice.'

'Then what are you worrying about?'

She shrugged and dabbed her eyes, and I got up and sat on the arm of her chair and put my arm round her shoulder. We had another cup of tea. She cheered up and said, 'I'm paid very well.'

'So that's how you've been able to make this place like the Waldorf?'

She laughed and nodded.

'Well, then I'm delighted.'

'You're a good lass.'

'Is it male or female? The tenant?'

'She's a girl.'

'Nice?'

'A real gem!'

'What's her name?'

'Vasha.'

'Pretty name. Is she pretty?'

'Not so pretty as you.'

I told Mrs Luxford that she wasn't going to flatter me out of my back bedroom. I wiped my fingers on my napkin.

'When shall I meet her? Vasha?'

'I never know. She works all sorts of hours.'

'Not another one at Pendragon?'

'Her boy-friend does. But not her, no. They wouldn't let *her*. Stands to reason. She's foreign.'

I reminded Mrs Luxford that to a Cornish Jack anyone east of the Tamar Bridge was a foreigner. She shook her head. 'Proper foreign. Czech.'

'A refugee?'

'That's right. She was a student over here in '68. Didn't go back when the Russians went in.'

'I'm not surprised.' I was ashamed of my momentary disappointment over the room.

Mrs Luxford got up. We moved towards the hall. She led the way up the narrow staircase.

'Been doing hotel work ever since.'

'Is that what she's doing now?'

'Yes.' She paused halfway up the stairs to get her breath. 'At the White Horse in St Edzell's. In the bar. A star attraction, you might say.'

'Who's her boy-friend?'

'Driver. Good job. Not a bad chap.'

'How about a house?' I said, teasing.

'Not at present.'

We paused on the landing. There were the four doors. Mrs Luxford's, the bathroom, the new girl's room, and mine.

'Like to peep in a moment? For old time's sake? Vasha won't mind.'

I shrugged. I didn't really want to. I don't like prying. But Mrs Luxford turned the handle and threw open the door. My old room was transformed. New white furniture, new bed. Everything neat and in apple-pie order. Only the big window and the view of the sea remained the same. I walked over the new cord carpet, rested my hands on the sill. From here on a fine day you could see from Land's End on one side to the Lizard on the other, and count every ship of any size in between. This evening in the hazing pinky-purple light, I saw a little flotilla of trawlers, silhouetted on the horizon.

The sea was calm. Everything was peaceful. I ached to have the feel of that firm moist sand under my feet. I wanted to digest my little homecoming. Besides, it was stifling in my old room with the window tightly bolted.

'Go for a walk? Yes, do that, m'dear. It'll do you good.' She glanced round Vasha's room again and shut the door.

'When William does get a house,' she said, speaking more to herself than me, 'it's my belief they'll be married and off. She'll have what she wants. She'll be as English as you or me.'

She was smiling. But there was something in her voice that told me all wasn't well. I was suddenly reminded of those huge radar scanners that heard things and saw things that no human ear and eye could see or hear. I thought, there are also such things in the voices of old friends.

It wasn't until just on six that I managed to get away. Mrs Luxford had taken me into the back bedroom, pointed out the pretty wallpaper, the good quality carpet, the hand-crocheted coverlet on the bed. I'd said the room was lovely. I'd leaned on the sill and admired the view across the tidy back garden, the new highway and the moor, with just in the extreme top right-hand corner like an artist's signature the wrong way up, a curve of high concrete posts that marked the south-western perimeter of the Pendragon Complex.

But for all my exclamations and admirations, I was disappointed. I didn't want this room. Its smallness hemmed me in. And I didn't want Vasha. I wanted everything to be the same as before. An indefinable feeling of unease came over me. I wanted to get out of the house, on to the headland, down to the sea – the sea that always changed and never changes.

I slipped a sweater over my shirt, and still in my black velvet pants, calling out to Mrs Luxford getting supper ready in the kitchen that I wouldn't be long, hurried down the path and on to the lane.

There were heavy banks of cloud to the west split with liquid apricot light, so Mrs Luxford was going to be right about the rain. The tide was up, with a heavy ground swell, and a strong neap current running in.

Halfway down, the lane bends right to join the main road. I stopped and searched in the hedge for the beginning of the path across the neck of Trethyddion Head that gives a short-cut to the Bay.

I looked back at the cottage. It stood out by itself on the headland like some jazzed-up lighthouse. I remember thinking wryly that Mrs Luxford couldn't have made it more conspicuous if she'd tried. Then I found the rusted mine tracks that form the stile and clambered over.

I thrust my way through brambles and sea gorse and tamarisk. It looked as though no one had come this way since I did three years ago. Yet this was the path the excise men and smugglers used to take, and then the coastguards, and in their day the miners looking for silver, tin and copper on the coast stopes.

Now peewits screamed up at the unaccustomed interruption. A hare, that legendary harbinger of so many of Mr Luxford's stories, bounded ahead of me, and then disappeared in the heather at the top of the cliff edge where the steps lead down.

The cliff here is about two hundred feet high. This is the curly, craggy part of Cornwall. The coast is crimped into tiny coves, crevasses, caves and islands, carved into strange shapes by the sea, with strange evocative names like the Gull, the Wild Horse, the Dead Duke, the Praying Maiden. There they were ahead of me now, one behind the other as they had been for thousands of years. Fortress walls, rising sheer up from the sea, their granite faces tinted amber in the last rays of this day's sun.

A rapidly fading sun paled to a yellow sky stain. Far away, the ruined stack and engine-house of Wheal Fortune stood out against it like a black felt collage, the giant whim no bigger than a French filigree button.

I put my hand on the heather and scrambled on to the first step. They are carved out of a natural chimney, slippery and scooped out in the middle by many feet. Cool air lapped round my feet like rising water. I jumped down the last three and on to the sand. It gave gently. I took off my shoes and fastened them round my pocket and walked the few steps to the edge of the sea. The tide had just turned.

The froth filtered gently in between my toes, the small waves from the ebbing tide splashed against my ankles. All round my feet were clustered Cornish pebbles polished smooth by the sea – granite and slate and quartz and serpentine. I bent down, my eyes searching for jasper and opal and citrine and amethyst, just as Mr Luxford and I used to do. All around me now were familiar places. I used to swim out to those rocks in the bay. Behind that granite buttress in the cliff side we used to shelter from the south-west winds. We used to search for crabs along that strip of soft wet sand. We used to hide in those shallow caves, now violet-mouthed in the evening light.

There was not a soul in sight, but the familiarity of it all drove out any feelings of loneliness. The sun had disappeared. But over on the southern horizon, the stars had come out, matched by the little brooches of lights on the trawlers. Looking at my watch, I saw it was almost half-past seven – well past time to be on my way back to Mrs Luxford's and supper.

Reluctantly I washed the sand off my feet, dried them with my handkerchief, put on my socks and shoes, and turned away from the sea to go back to the steps.

It was then that I saw it.

A weirdly formed piece of rock, that was my first impression.

I walked three steps nearer.

It was a trick of this deceiving light. That jet black shininess was some kind of reflection off the sea.

I walked forward another three slow steps. The sand here was sticky. It clung to my feet. But each step inexorably solidified the shape out of the darkness.

A head. A body. Webbed feet. A dead seal washed up and abandoned by the receding tide.

I took two more steps towards it. Then I saw the half-human shape. Black rubber arms, aqualung equipment, two metal cylinders strapped to the back, the black-capped head on its side in the sand, the goggles smashed and broken.

The diver was lying on the beach, his flippered feet still trailing in the shallow water where the last big wave had just cast him up. He lay effortlessly, without struggle, as if he had been a long time dead.

For seconds I stood there frozen. When I did force myself forward, the sand glued my feet like steps in a nightmare. My breath gulped in my throat. Those few steps were like climbing a mountain. I thought even then: I'll wake up soon. The thing will have gone. Someone will come.

I reached his side. I forced myself to kneel down. I forced myself to touch him, to feel his reality with another sense. The arm was cold to the touch, heavy as lead. I dragged back the cuff with scrabbling trembling hands. A bitter fluid rushed into my mouth. I had to pause a moment to stop my own trembling. Then I let my fingers listen for his pulse.

Nothing.

The thick wrist was sodden and heavy. I might as well have felt for a pulse in a potter's 'slip'.

I dropped his arm. It fell with a squelchy thud. I dragged off the mask, unlatched the buckles of the cylinders, straddled the huge cold back, kneaded my hands into the unyielding rib cage.

There was a grunting, gurgling noise. A quick foul gush of slimy water out of his lungs and stomach. I released the pressure, pressed down again. In and out. On and on.

There was no further response, nothing. In desperation, using all my strength, I pushed at the rubbery body, managed to move it, heave it over on to its back. He lay, arms outflung. Dead. Abused somehow by my clumsy handling of him. Probably dead for hours. Jaw agape. Wide eyes turned to the sky, filmed over like kidneys. A brown beard, the colour of seaweed. Blue blubbery lips.

I leaned over and rested my head against the cold barrel chest. Not a sign of life. Not the slightest tremor of a heart-beat. I stretched over further. I pressed my lips to those cold blubbery ones. I breathed out, drew in. I retched. Went on breathing. In and out, in and out. To the time of the turning waves, then to the words in my brain. A night-mare. Wake soon.

I don't know how long I tried. I became aware that the white water's edge was now fifty yards away. It was a black night and raining hard. My hair clung to my forehead. Tears or sweat or rain dribbled down my cheeks. My neck ached. My lips felt sore. Gritty with something on the dead man's mouth. I scrubbed them with my handkerchief.

I got stiffly to my feet. I could hear the rain dropping into the tide pools, and faintly and far away, the thrum of cars along the highway. Headlights reflected momentarily on the cloud like harvest lightning.

I thrust my feet into my shoes. I began to run up the beach, shouting as I went. I passed a great wedge-shaped rock, a pile of boulders, a scatter of stones. All of them had grown eyes and ears and arms. I still half expected to wake up. I was panting when I reached the foot of the cliff. As I started the climb up towards the headlights on the main road, I looked back.

The diver's body lay as I had left it, unmoving as the rocks.

I ran across the road, waving at the first car. It went sweep-ing past. A face stared back from the rear window, its expression astonished, disdainful. I remembered my torn pants, windblown hair, torn filthy shirt.

I took no chances with the next. I stood out full in front of it, flapping my arms, screwing my eyes up against its headlights. It slowed, drew into the kerb – a black MG. There was a second's pause. I was being observed. Then the driver leaned across, opened the passenger door. I opened my mouth to gabble a frantic explanation.

'Get in!' The man spoke with an antiseptic sharpness. I was only halfway through the door when the car began to move.

'Don't go yet!'

But he had already closed the door and begun accelerating.

'There's a body. A man. Down there on the beach.'

'Who?'

'I don't know.'

It was too dark to see the driver's face clearly. But I knew he was looking at me intently. 'Is he dead?'

'Yes.'

'You're sure?'

I nodded.

'How?'

I gabbled out the story.

'He was in diving gear, you say?'

The needle on the speedometer swept past sixty.

'Yes.'

I drew a deep breath. 'Don't you think we ought to take a look?'

'Go down to the beach, you mean?'

'Yes.'

'Too long.'

'Then shouldn't we telephone? I'm staying at a cottage a couple of miles back.'

'There's a telephone-box just before St Edzell's.' Now the needle on the speedometer was nudging ninety. 'And as he's dead . . .' He tightened his lips. Two or three cars passed us, coming in the opposite direction. I glanced at his profile in the flick of their headlights. It told me very little. A face to match his voice. A closed-up, taut kind of face – helpful or unhelpful, trustworthy or untrustworthy, I wouldn't know.

'Must have been a shock for you,' he said suddenly, as if aware of something I sought from him.

'Yes.'

'Still, you seem to have taken it all right.' A flick of a sideways glance. 'Done all you could.'

I shrugged, pressing my knees together to keep my body from shaking. 'I wonder who he was?'

'The police'll find out.' Not much sympathy there. 'That's their job. What's your name?'

'Olivia Browning.' We were past the intersection now where one curve of concrete ribbon swept up over the moor. Over on the right a halo of blue-white neon illuminated the naval airfield complex.

'Live here?'

'No. Just staying.' I laughed shakily. 'For a holiday. And you . . . ?'

'My name's Jim Curtis. I don't live here either.'

'I hope I'm not taking you out of your way.'

Under the circumstances, it sounded silly even to me. He glanced at me sideways again. But he said nothing.

We began rounding a bend. The needle on the speedometer fell back sharply. There was a sudden screech of brakes, squeal of tyres.

We had stopped outside a telephone-box.

'Won't be a moment.' He began feeling in his pockets.

'Let the police know we're coming.'

'Dial 999,' I said. 'You don't need coins.'

He said nothing.

He got out, crossed in front of the car, paused in the headlights to examine the loose change in his hand. Thirty, maybe thirty-five. Dark hair, thick black brows. I am categorizing him like a police description, I remember thinking, smiling to myself with the hysterical amusement that follows shock. I watched his tall figure move unhurriedly yet somehow swiftly into the phone-box.

The door shut behind him. He turned his back towards me.

I wound down the window – not just for fresh air. He was a long time getting through.

I glanced round the car, the way one idly glances round any stranger's habitat, wondering what he did, what was his job, where he was going. The interior was new, clean, immaculate – but already there was 43,105 miles on the clock. And on the dashboard was the handsomest and most complicated car radio I'd ever seen.

I leaned right out of the window, and felt the cold night air on my forehead. I heard the ping of a coin in the box. Mr Curtis, if that was his name, still had his back towards me.

Then he was coming out, striding towards me. He opened the car door. There was a slight rueful smile, as he settled himself into the driver's seat and started up. 'Damn the Post Office!'

'Couldn't you get through?'

We moved forward sedately.

'Not a peep.'

'Was it broken?'

Slowly he eased the car back into the main stream.

'Yes.' He tucked himself behind a lorry, made no attempt to pass. The needle on the speedometer registered a sedate thirty. 'That's the way it is these days. Vandals.'

'Out here?'

Again my tone made him turn. A faint smile. 'The further away the better.' He sighed. Thick black brows drawn together, arched, humorously rueful. 'Ton-up kids on bikes.'

The lorry driver waved us on. We *had* to pass. Curtis concentrated on the road.

'I thought you seemed to be talking to someone.'

'I was.' He laughed. 'Myself. Cursing like hell!'

A quick silence between us. Only the swish of the tyres on the smooth concrete, the thump of the joins, the soft unstrained hum of the engine, and the thrum of cars in the opposite direction. Then very softly, 'You're an observant girl.'

'Not particularly.' My knees still shook. I clasped my hands as if to hold my body together.

'After shock, people often . . .' A small grey van overtook us. He glanced down at my clenched hands. '. . . forget the important, remember only the details.'

'Yes.'

'A day or so later, things fall into perspective.'

I didn't answer. I wondered why he was talking like this. Or was he for that matter, talking in any special way? Wasn't he being simply the cool but kind stranger? Not overdoing the sympathy or the drama. Putting things, exactly as he had said, into perspective.

Another half a mile – the speedometer needle never going above thirty. With a clear road, why this sudden dawdling?

Ahead now, the lights of St Edzell's. We branched off the new highway, on to a dark road, high-hedged and narrow.

Thorn branches scraped on the side of the car. A mizzling rain had begun.

'Cornwall!' Curtis switched on the windscreen wiper. 'The fine weather's a myth.' The rueful laugh again. 'So you're on holiday too?'

'Yes.'

'Hope we're not stuck with this sort of stuff.'

We were dropping down Beacon Hill into the town. The road straightened, the hedges vanished. He glanced out at the flat black that was the sea on our right. On the left rows of villas, rigid and reassuring as ranks of soldiers, lined the road. Curtained windows glowed. Television screens flickered behind undrawn windows. A line of shops – new ones. A supermarket, still open. The old cinema – now a Bingo Hall. A queue of people waiting outside. We drove on, down to the promenade. Summer illuminations still garlanded the lamp-posts. Pink and blue butterflies, peacocks, roses, fleurs-de-lys. A few late holidaymakers strolled along the road.

Curtis slowed to a crawl.

'Don't want another casualty,' he said, sensing my impatience.

There was a covered Fun Fair close by. I could hear the bang of the Dodgems, piped music, the howl of the top-speed klaxon. I could smell fish and chips and candy floss.

He turned sharp right. At least he knew his way. We came to a halt under a blue pendant light.

We got out of the car, walked up three steps. I remember wondering if they made all police stations alike. The usual corridor lined with police notices – crop-pest warnings to farmers, two photos of Wanted Men, a poster for a police charity ball. The usual half-frosted inner door. The usual sort of counter. Like a pub without the bonhomie and the smell of beer. The usual sort of sergeant, thick necked, scrubbed, cautiously affable. The usual bright hard neon light glittered on the usual silver chain to the usual whistle in his top pocket. I fixed my eyes steadfastly on that whistle as though to hypnotize myself back into normality.

Curtis was doing the talking. As he listened, the policeman's eyes flickered over me. I could feel them, feel where they paused, feel where something he found important clicked inside his computerized brain.

'The body of a man?'

I nodded.

'Drowned?'

I nodded.

'On which beach, miss?'

Curtis wouldn't know the name, I thought. I would have to speak. My lower lip trembled.

'Trethyddion. I picked her up there. I imagine . . .'

His voice seemed to fade. He was still going on. But I could hardly hear him. He was someone talking at the end of a long corridor, a mannikin figure at the wrong end of a telephone.

I clenched my teeth. I *would* speak.

'Yes, Trethyddion,' a high female voice said. Mine. The floor of the office was tilting steeply. If I moved an inch I would go sliding down. I clenched my hands tight.

'She's whitish, sir.'

The silver chain had moved. The hypnotic effect was broken.

'Shock, Officer.'

I felt hands on my shoulder. Fingers pressed hard. There was a squeak of a chair across the floor. There was some talk of telephoning for an ambulance. My whole body broke out into a cold sweat. But as if it were a fever passed, my senses cleared. I was aware I was sitting beside a table now, a map spread out before me. A yellow mug of tea had been produced. It sat on the blue of the English Channel within reach of my hand. I sipped a little – lukewarm and too sweet.

'That better, miss?'

'Yes, Sergeant.'

'Well, then, if you wouldn't mind.' He began filling in a form. 'Just a few questions. Name?'

'Olivia Browning.'

'Age?'

'Twenty-five.'

'Marital state?'

'Single.'

'Address?'

'Twenty-five, Park Place, Kensington.'

'Now would that be a flat, miss?'

'Yes.'

'Share it with anyone . . . another young lady I mean, miss?'

'No.'

'Occupation, miss?'

'Conservationist.'

'And what would that be, miss?'

'I touch up old paintings, ceramics, that sort of thing.'

'Next of kin, miss?'

I wanted to get up and shout *I'm* not the body, I only found it. But I hadn't the strength to protest. So, meekly, apologetically almost, 'I haven't any over here.'

Curtis and the sergeant glanced at me sharply. As if the absence of relatives was suspicious in itself. 'Where then, miss?'

'My father's in South America. Chile.'

'Mother?'

'Dead. My father re-married.'

'Have you no brothers or sisters, Miss Browning?' Curtis asked me.

I shook my head.

'And for why did you come to St Edzell's, miss?'

'Partly a holiday. Partly to see an old friend.' I told them about Mrs Luxford.

The sergeant wrote it all down laboriously. Curtis thrust his hands in his pockets, watched me through narrowed eyes.

'And when did you arrive, miss? At Trethyddion Cottage?'

'This afternoon.'

'How did you come, miss? By train or bus or car or what?'

'Car.'

'Yours?'

'Yes.'

'What's its number, miss?'

'GHK 348H. A Triumph Coupé. 1970.'

'Did you drive all the way today, miss?'

'Yes.'

'Where did you stop for lunch?'

'I didn't.'

'Best to have a proper meal, I always say, miss. Makes you faintish unless. Were you weary when you got here?'

'No.'

'Then did you go straight on the beach when you arrived?'

'After tea.'

'For an evening stroll, eh, miss?'

'Yes.'

'And you'd been walking how long when you found this diver's body, miss?'

'An hour, maybe more.'

'You must've been weary *then*, miss?'

'Not really.'

'And it was dusk, miss, was it? Or dark?'

'Dusk.'

'Nasty old light that, miss.' Voice becoming confidential. 'We get more accidents then than any time.'

I said nothing.

'The light's deceiving, miss.'

'Yes.'

'Now can you describe this diver, this fellow, miss?'

I closed my eyes. I tried to focus my mind's eye on that fearful imprint. One would think it would be cut deep into my memory. But as Curtis said, shock does strange things. My mind refused. The face blurred. I could remember only those terrible blubbery lips, and the wispy beard.

'Big mouth, thick lips,' I said. 'Brownish hair, a beard.'

'Old or young?'

'Middle-aged.'

'Fat sort of fellow like me? Or tall and slim like Mr Curtis?'

'Like neither. I don't really know. Thick-set. Difficult to say how tall. He was lying flat. Why don't you go and see for yourselves?'

'Presently. It's all arranged, miss.'

Then Curtis interceding again, 'How was he lying, Miss Browning?'

I described it as best I could. 'Diagonally across the sand. Washed up by the current. Feet in the water. The current's strong there.' A look exchanged over my head. 'At first I thought it was a rock.'

'Yes, miss.' A smile, a pregnant pause. 'Did he have any identification on him? Rings? Gold fillings to his teeth? Tattoo marks? Scars? Such like, miss?'

'I don't know.'

'Could he have been foreign?'

'I suppose so. How can one tell?'

'He didn't say anything?'

'He was dead.'

I clasped my hands in front of me. The picture briefly refocused in my mind. There were several things that worried me about it. Fragments that weren't right. Like the tiny faults that can tell an expert a picture is a fake. But I couldn't identify them.

'Did he look foreign, miss?'

I shrugged.

And as if excusing my ignorance, the sergeant said, 'Don't get abroad much, I suppose?'

'Quite a bit.'

'Where?' Curtis asked conversationally.

I named a few places. I felt hot and clammy cold alternatively. I felt in my pocket for my hankie. Couldn't find it.

Why didn't they get a move on?

'Were these holidays, miss? Seeing old friends again?'

'The Sofia trip was to buy an ikon. I went with the museum director. We didn't know how much touching up it would need.'

'And his name and address. The director?'

'What on earth has that got to do with this? Please. Go and get that body. The body.' I tried to stand up. Curtis's hand descended on my shoulder.

'Tell him, Miss Browning. Everything helps. You might be called for the Inquest. Delayed going back. Besides, we've got to wait for the ambulance and lifting tackle.'

'Mr Laski, the Bullingham Museum and Art Gallery. Knightsbridge.'

'Foreign is he, miss? Laski? Name like that.' The sergeant had foreigners on the brain.

'Jewish.'

'Sorry, miss. No offence meant.'

'It helps to have a foreign name in the art world.'

'Really, miss?' The sergeant looked disbelieving.

'I know the museum,' Curtis put in smoothly. 'Have you worked there long?'

'About a year. And before that,' I anticipated their question, 'I was at the V and A.'

'Got your passport, have you, miss?'

'No. Why should I have?' I looked down at my empty hands. There was blood on them from the climb up the cliff. I hadn't remembered feeling them sore at the time.

'Where is it?'

'Back in my flat.'

'Have you any means of identification?'

I shook off Curtis's restraining hand and stood up. Anger stiffened me. 'It's not me you should be worrying about. For God's sake, get to that poor chap on the beach.'

'But you said he was dead, miss.'

'Yes, but . . .'

'Can't do anything for him.'

'The body. Won't the sea . . .'

'Tide's going out, miss.' He took a long sip of his tea. 'Big beach, Trethyddion. *Where* do you say you found it, miss?'

I got up. 'I'll show you. Let's go and I'll *show* you.'

'You're upset, miss.' Out in the street a klaxon sounded. 'There's the ambulance now.'

Doors opened. There was a lot of coming and going of uniformed men, and finally, as if hastily summoned, a policewoman whom they all addressed as Madge. She was black-haired, young and pretty. I wondered why they wanted her at all.

A smell of gusty sea air blew in. It was still raining hard. I glimpsed the white side of the ambulance. Its flickering blue roof light reflected on the wet street.

'Are you going to come with us then, miss?'

'I think she should stay with me.' Curtis's hand held my arm. The sergeant didn't argue. The lights from the police station flung our conjoined shadow ahead.

Gaoler and gaoled. I shook my arm free. I saw Curtis smile at my token independence.

'Here,' I said.

Curtis braked. 'Sure?'

'Sure.'

'Thought it was a bit further up.' He stopped all the same. Behind us, the ambulance and the police car stopped too.

Curtis led the way through the rain to the clump of men.

'. . . she says she's sure.'

'Can't get down to Trethyddion from here, miss.' The sergeant's voice.

I walked over to the short scrub of grass on the side of the road. A few yards beyond was a sheer cliff edge.

'Sign you up on the next Everest expedition, miss.' The sergeant again.

'Easy to make a mistake. Dark.' Curtis's voice.

'You're right,' I said. 'It must be a bit further up.'

We went on another half mile. 'Wasn't it here?' Curtis said.

I nodded. We got out again. It *was* here. Now I remembered the gorse bushes and the shaly sand. The cliff again, but not so sheer in the light of the torches.

'Nasty old climb,' the sergeant said. 'Must've taken it out of you.'

My eyes were getting used to the dark. Below I could see

the white froth of the sea's edge. We began the descent. Curtis produced a torch, the beam fingering the stone outcrops ahead.

Gingerly we made our way down. First pebbly shingle, then a slaty scree, running with water. Further along boulders, crusted with barnacles, ribboned with weed, and in between the wet yielding sand. This was near the place.

I stopped.

'Anything the matter, miss?'

'No.'

I was looking around for my footprints.

There was no sign of them. The whole beach looked as if it had been washed clean as a wet slate. But I could see the wedge-shaped rock. I pointed.

'Over there.'

Slowly we squelched our way towards it – the sergeant, two policemen, a policewoman, the ambulance men, Curtis, me.

'Where, miss?'

'Near here.'

More torches were produced. Yellow beams like little searchlights criss-crossed the dripping granite.

'Sure, miss?'

'Of course I'm sure.'

'Then where is it, miss?'

Just a fur of drenched green seaweed over the wedge-shaped rock. In a tiny pool, shells glittered, an anemone glowed.

'It *must* be here.'

'He was dead, miss?'

'He was dead.'

'Couldn't have got up and walked away then, miss.'

'Then somebody else must've – '

'But why, miss?'

Nobody said anything. More torchlight. More searching.

Nothing there, except the rain and the night and the soft sigh of the sea.

I looked round the faces. All blank. All closed up against me.

Nobody said anything. I said nothing either. I went on looking, in a flustered, disorganized way as if a body could be hidden underneath seaweed or in thin crevices.

And then someone, Curtis I think it was, pointed out the faint imprints of my bare feet. My feet only. No mark of a body. Just that faint wavy line – all that was left after that intervening hour or so of continuous rain.

'Barefoot, miss? On this wet cold night?'

I nodded. I was too tired to explain.

There was another long silence. A poor mad thing, I could hear them thinking. Ophelia rather than Olivia.

Finally Curtis said in a kindly soothing voice, 'Well, look here, you must be absolutely exhausted. These chaps'll see to whatever has to be done. I'll drive you home.'

We walked back up through the drenching rain to the cars and the ambulance. Curtis was right. I was tired, dispirited, cold. In a way frightened, too. We said goodnight to the others. Sweeping back along the main road, Curtis drove very fast. I told him where to slow up for the turning. He didn't slacken much. We skidded round the corner and up the lane.

Lights were shining all over the cottage. Mrs Luxford must be in a panic. I was glad we weren't in a police car. She hurried down the path under a big umbrella as soon as she saw the headlights. I was too tired now to open my mouth and waited for Curtis to do the explanations. But few seemed to be necessary.

'The sergeant gave me a tinkle,' she said. 'Dear oh, dear oh, dear. What a thing to happen!'

We went inside.

Shock and stress made Mrs Luxford garrulous. I leaned against the wall. Past and present blurred. The refracted light on her spectacles turned to the eyepiece on the dead diver's face. Voices swelled and faded. I heard Curtis's voice saying very loud, 'I think she should go to bed.' I felt his hand on my arm again. He was helping me up the stairs. Mrs Luxford was calling up that she'd laid my dressing-gown on the bed, and would bring up a cup of Ovaltine.

He opened the door for me, switched on the light, drew the curtains. All unhurried. For a moment as I sat on the corner of the bed, he stood looking down at me, a strange expression on his face. 'Sure you'll be all right now? Don't think about it any more. Put it all out of your mind. Tell yourself it never happened.'

I nodded and thanked him. I watched him shut my bedroom door softly behind him.

Seconds later I heard Mrs Luxford saying goodnight to him, and the MG go hurtling down the lane like a bat out of hell.

That night, an unburied corpse, the dead diver haunted me. Gone from Trethyddion Beach, he was here in my room. Now stretched near my window, now struggling to his feet, hand on my door.

The Ovaltine was still untouched. I could hear the new clock in the living-room chiming the hours. Twelve o'clock. One o'clock. Two o'clock. Then footsteps on the stairs, up to the landing. The scrape of a lock. The door to my old room opening and closing.

Vasha, the unknown. Certainly a late-night girl.

Handfuls of rain rattled on the glass. A slight wind trembled the frame. It seemed like some feeble attempt of *something* to get in. I pulled the bedcovers over my head. I felt desperately tired, but my mind and memory were crystal clear. It was as if, simultaneously, I could see both what I knew had happened and what the police obviously thought had happened. As if I would mistake a rock for a dead diver. As if I would straddle it, attempt to revive it, roll it over, give it the kiss of life . . .

Weakly, just after it had chimed three, out of the sheer frustration of communicating the truth to anyone, I started to cry. Then I must have drifted off to sleep. And the nightmare began.

I was drowning deep in an unfathomable blackness of water. Far away a blue-white light flickered. An engine hummed. I couldn't decide whether I had to struggle towards it or avoid it. All I knew was that my lungs were bursting and I was going to die. Then Mr Curtis had hold of my arm. I turned to see his face. It had changed to that of the drowned man. Soft sodden limbs enfolded me. Swollen lips pressed on mine. I tasted grit, salt water, vomit.

I retched, screamed, went on screaming.

Now full in the light, Mrs Luxford in a faded blue dressing-gown, hair in curlers, her little stubby hands pulling back the bedclothes from my face. She clicked her tongue, murmured soothingly. And yet behind the concern in her eyes, a diagnostic look like the sergeant's. 'Shall I get the doctor, Livvy love?' Her childish name for me. My eyes filled with tears. 'Get him to give you something to sleep?'

'I'm all right.' I ran my hand through my hair. 'I had a bad dream, that's all.'

I actually smiled. I felt better. He had been dead, I remember thinking. I had done all I could. Nothing else would have brought him back to life. 'I seemed to see lights . . . hear engines.'

'That blessed Navy airfield!' She tweaked the curtains, clicked her tongue. 'I should've given you your old room, after all.'

'I'm fine now. Just a dream.'

'That's right. There's nothing to be afraid of.' The blind leading the blind. The fearful leading the fearful. 'Go to sleep now, Livvy . . . like a good girl.'

She closed the door softly. I heard her bedroom slippers slip-slop against the back of her heels as she went along the corridor to her own room.

The cottage settled into silence. The rain had stopped. Not a sound from Vasha's room. I wondered if she had heard me, been puzzled, even frightened. Or perhaps she was used to hearing people cry out in the night, and had learned to stay quiet and say nothing.

Friday

I woke to the smell of coffee, plates rattling, water running, helicopters overhead making the most of a fine, clear morning. I heard Mrs Luxford humming hymns to herself as she hung out the washing in the back garden. I dressed and went downstairs. The door to the living-room was open. The Czech girl sat with her back to it. But she knew about the uses of the gilt-framed mirror over the mantelpiece. She had already sized me up before I came into the room, while all I could see of her were sloping shoulders, generous hips, and a mass of ash-blonde hair.

She turned her head slowly and smiled, rested a graceful arm on the back of her chair. 'It can be no other than Olivia.' A faint mischievous deepening of the smile.

I smiled back. 'And you're Vasha. I've heard a lot about you, too.'

We looked each other over. My own feeling was of slight surprise. No Slavonic sloe-eyed beauty, this. No husky-voiced mystery out of some old Garbo film. She had an oval boneless face – the kind you see dozens of in any English town. English enough, I remember thinking, to satisfy even the xenophobic police sergeant. Only Vasha's eyes singled her out. They were large, full and golden-brown, their size exaggerated by black shadow and long false lashes. She had a small gay mouth and a lovely long neck.

She stood up and held out both her hands. She was smaller than me. She kissed me on each cheek. The curious eyes sparkled. 'I know we shall be great friends,' she said. 'It is nice to have someone my own age.' She spoke charmingly in a light clear voice with a slight lisp and a slight accent. I could see why she was the star attraction at the White Horse. 'Now Mother Luxford has given me strict instructions. Your breakfast is in the warming oven. You are to eat it all up. Every scrap.'

I went into the kitchen and took out the plateful of bacon and eggs. I called good morning through the window to Mrs Luxford. Her mouth was full of pegs. She looked at me with concern but waved back gaily.

'Shut the door, please,' Vasha said. 'I am not quite so enthusiastic for fresh air as Mother Luxford.'

'Where do you come from in Czechoslovakia?'

'Brno.'

'Doesn't it get pretty cold there?'

'A *different* cold.' She smiled, and pushed out a chair for me with her foot. 'Come and sit down, and tell me you forgive me.'

'For what?'

'For taking your room.'

'Oh, *that*. There's nothing to forgive. I'm very comfortable where I am.'

She leaned over the table. 'Yet you did not sleep well.'

'Did I wake you? I'm so sorry.'

'No, no. I soon sleep deep again.'

I said nothing, and still with her eyes on my face she poured me a cup of coffee and passed it over.

'It was nothing to do with the room,' I said.

'What was it then, Olivia?'

I cut up my bacon and eggs, but the smell revolted me and I didn't lift my fork to my mouth.

'Was it to do with the man you found?' She held up her hand. 'Mother Luxford told me a little this morning. I am all horror.' The ash-blonde hair quivered with sympathy. She clicked her tongue. Coaxingly, 'Please tell me about it.'

I gave her the bare bones of last night's story. I finished up by saying, 'At least, that's what I *think* happened.'

In the cool clear light of morning it all seemed rather bizarre. I was losing confidence in my own perceptions. One thing about art is that it teaches you a lot about illusion. What does the artist make you see but one big illusion? It was beginning to enter my mind that I might have fallen victim to my own illusion, to something which a psychiatrist would say was buried deep in my subconscious, awaiting the right combination of circumstances to bring out.

I was therefore inordinately grateful for Vasha's obvious belief.

'But how *terrible*! What a dreadful experience! I did not gather from Mother Luxford that it was like that.' Vasha's voice trailed. She dipped into her skirt pocket and brought out a packet of cigarettes.

She looked at my untouched breakfast. 'Are you going to eat that?'

I shook my head.

'Have a cigarette. Do you more good. Don't let Mother Luxford see, though.' She went quickly through into the kitchen, came back with a bag, scraped the plate into it. 'Feed it to the gulls. They will be hungry.'

She took out a lighter and lit our cigarettes.

'What did you gather from Mrs Luxford?' I asked.

'That he, this thing, was either a . . .' she snapped her fingers, 'walrus.'

'Seal, you mean?'

'Yes.'

I shook my head. 'It wasn't.'

'Or this diver was not dead. He got up and walked away. Swam maybe?'

'He was dead all right.'

She smoked in silence for a moment. Then leaned across the table. Her eyes shone as if with unshed tears, 'I have seen dead people, but have you?'

'Yes.'

A pause. She nodded as if I had satisfied her. She drew on her cigarette. 'And they did not find any sign of who he was, the police?'

'I don't think they tried. They didn't believe me.'

She puffed fiercely. 'I do not believe in *them*. Corrupt, all of them.'

'They're usually pretty fair, the British police,' I said in all justice.

'Police *nowhere* are fair! It is not in their nature. Jack-booted jackasses. Everywhere.'

She lapsed into some angry reverie. The gay mouth thinned. Coming back to the present suddenly, she asked me what the diver looked like. I felt more relaxed than last night, and I remembered the face with less revulsion. I described him, his face, his build, his suit.

'And do you think he drowned?'

'His lungs were full of water. So I suppose he did.'

'There were no violent marks on him then?'

'None.'

'And how did he lie? This man in the sand?'

'Half on his side. Diagonally. As if the current had brought him in.'

'There is a strong current there?'

'Yes. Terribly strong. Especially at this time of the year.'

'And he was very dead? Maybe an hour? More?'

I nodded.

'So he perhaps died somewhere else?'

'I suppose so.' I drew deeply on the cigarette. 'I don't know. I don't really understand any of it.'

'Nor do I, Livvy. One thing especially I do not understand. How would a diver drown? What could have happened? What misfortune could have overtaken him?'

I shook my head. Vasha pushed back her chair. 'Poor man, he is dead, whatever happened. And now I must go.' She looked at her watch. 'My employers at the White Horse will be shrinking my pay packet.'

From the kitchen there came the sprightly humming of 'Lead us Heavenly Father', the rattle of the peg box.

'Hide your breakfast bag, friend Livvy. Here comes Mother Luxford.'

The door from the kitchen opened. Immediately Mrs Luxford's eyes scanned my plate.

'See, Mother Luxford, what an excellent breakfast Livvy has eaten.' A different, gayer Vasha winked at me as she went towards the stairs.

I followed.

'What is a little white lie,' she said as if I might reproach her. 'When already you and I are such good friends.'

'Well, Livvy,' Mrs Luxford said briskly, when Vasha had gone, 'feel all right, do you, this morning?'

I had a stiffness in my neck, and my hands were grazed. That was all. I said I felt fine. To my relief, Mrs Luxford wore her hat. She was securing the veil with a big pearl-tipped pin.

'And what did you think of doing with yourself today?' She unhooked a shopping-bag from behind the kitchen door. She was off, she said, to St Edzell's to do the weekend marketing. There was a ladies' lunch in the Chapel hall with a speaker afterwards. I could come with her or no according to my whim.

She refused my offer of a lift. She didn't press me to accompany her. I said I must unpack. Then perhaps take a walk, and as I'd brought my swimming things, maybe have a bathe.

'Not today, m'dear,' she sounded quite scandalized. 'The red flags are up. He's having exercises.'

Out at sea, about two miles to the south-west, was a red flag on a buoy. There was a red blipping beacon at the top of Liscawen Head. I watched three helicopters fly over the beacon and fan out over the square. They didn't drop anything. It looked like a jolly game of aerial hopscotch.

'What sort of things do they do on these exercises?'

'I don't rightly know, m'dear. They drop things. There's a nice gentleman at chapel and *he* works up there. Along at Pendragon. He says the less people know the better.'

'I bet.'

'Now William – Vasha's intended – he knows a lot.'

'D'you ever see what happens?'

'It's too far away usually, m'dear. Just once I did though.'

'Did it go off with a bang?'

'Not at all. Came down as gentle as you like, as if it were a puff of dandelion fluff.' She smiled. 'Ever so pretty really. Quite a nice sight.'

Obviously well worth a taxpayer's money, I thought wryly.

'It's really a testing station you see, m'dear.' Mrs Luxford looked troubled. 'Just for defence.'

'I see.'

'I wouldn't go down to the beach at all, Livvy, if I was you.'

'I thought I might look for some rose quartz.'

'You can find some near the adits. The upthrowing by

Wheal Cannock. It's a lovely walk down along and to Port Navar. And while you're there – ' she walked towards the door – 'you might get me some crabmeat fresh from the canning station. Like none other, it is, if you get it fresh.'

Satisfied that she had spun her gentle protective web around me, that I would find no more disappearing bodies, have no more hallucinations, she reminded me to lock the door behind me, adding that there was a leg of cold chicken for my lunch in the fridge, and to be sure and be home in good time for high tea.

I waved her off. I watched her disappear down the lane. I unpacked quickly. Then I searched around for what I'd worn last night. I intended to go over my clothes carefully to see if there was anything which would support my reviving belief in me. I couldn't find them anywhere. Then I looked out of the window. My velvet trousers and silk shirt were dancing in the wind on the washing-line between aprons and wool vests and Mrs Luxford's directoire drawers. There was no sign of my shoes.

I took out an anorak and went downstairs. My shoes were in the kitchen standing on a newspaper beside the range, meticulously cleaned.

Half over the metal stile, I paused for a moment with the wind in my face. On the left, the granite of the cliff, veined with serpentine, stretched round St Edzell's. High in the blue sky above, a white gull wheeled. The helicopters had gone. Now it was the turn of the little launches towing their white washes behind them to join the game, while beyond the glittering foreground on the horizon lay the muffled curls of trawler smoke as the fishermen went about the real business of the day.

I wasn't sure how I was going to go about it, but I was

alert for all clues. In the darkness and the rain, under impatient hostile eyes, it was easy to have missed something. I am not Cornish fey and that diver was no ghost. There must be something left – an imprint, a bit of the diving gear, a piece of the cracked goggles.

I jumped down on the other side, treading in yesterday's footprints down to the steps. The beach was in the headland's shadow and quite empty. The tide had rearranged the weed in fresh mounds. Down here there were no footprints left, just a scatter of little pools and ribs of sand. The sea and the rain between them had scavenged the whole place clean as Mrs Luxford's line of clothes. As far as Trethyddion Beach was concerned, what I and the police and Curtis had done only a few hours ago had vanished like the diver.

I retraced my approximate path. It is an odd feeling to find nothing of yourself at all. Here was the pool where I had picked up pebbles, quite undisturbed, exactly the same as I had first seen it. Ahead now was the wedge-shaped rock, surrounded by a frill of shallow seawater, but not a sign that we had scrambled all over it. I began methodically working from the exact spot where I thought the body had lain. I knelt down and examined the smooth coverlet of wet sand. I dug into it with my fingers, scooping back with the sides of my hands. I uncovered a strip of shiny brown weed, thick as a razor-strop, a broken scallop shell, a piece of driftwood, half a dozen flat pebbles, a skeleton fish head, a pink crab very much alive.

Nothing else.

Nothing else for fifty yards around the rock either. I searched every inch. Then I paced that beach from end to end right down to the water's edge, and still I found nothing. A fruitless search, and an aimless one too – not knowing what I was looking for, proof of my sanity perhaps in this tide-turned sand.

Surely, I thought, this cove cupped something more than just quiet. Surely life didn't disappear this quickly? Surely some scent of death would linger here, some awareness of tragedy?

But there was only the salt smell of the sea breeze, and the wet sand sparkling in the sunlight.

I remember standing at the far end of the bay, thinking 'It must be me. My horizontals and verticals are out of true. I cannot separate my thoughts, my imaginings, my memories from what I actually see and hear. I am like those people who send wreaths and baby clothes to soap opera characters. Only I am worse.' And then I lifted up my eyes from the sand to the empty headland – and there I saw it.

A small incongruous scrap of white, high up on the grey cliff side. The soft matt white of some crumpled material.

Back my mind flew to last night – cleaning the dead diver's face with my handkerchief. Not being able to find it down at the police station. In between, a blank. I couldn't remember what I had done with it. I had no recollection of putting it in my trouser pocket. That little patch of white *might* just be mine. If it was, at least that was a clue, something positive, a piece of last night that had managed to survive after all. Proof to me anyway, that I hadn't imagined it all. But how could it have got there – blown four hundred feet up, and as many yards to the south, when the winds had been so light? And *from* the south-west.

I didn't wait to work that one out. The first thing to do was to get up there and find out if it was my handkerchief. I ran over to the Head, round the tide pools and then up over the big granite base boulders that at least lessened the incline.

I began climbing. I worked my way sideways and up. I hauled myself on to a shaly ledge that sprouted some withered fern. It led to a sort of path winding up the headland.

I paused for breath there. It had been steeper than I thought. More nerve-racking too. I was above the sea now. Big smooth wave-heads ran in below my feet, broke in a sunlit froth over the rocks. Above, if I put my head back, I could see the scrap of white. A hundred feet or so above me. It *was* a handkerchief. I watched it fluttering a little, impaled on the spikes of a spindly gorse-bush. It seemed desperately important to me to get it, before it blew away again. I stepped on to the path. It was narrow and shaly.

Under my feet loose shells and pebbles careered down the cliff side. I climbed gingerly upwards. I crouched against the cliff face, grabbing every bit of jutting rock, placing each foot with care. There were little vertical screes where the path had weathered, making miniature landslides. Fifty yards on, the path became steeper, the side more sheer, with very little path left, only naked rock.

But the handkerchief was just above me – and it was mine. I could see its lace edging caught round a thorn. I inched my way forward, round a jutting outcrop, and up. There was a nasty three-foot gap in the granite, and then another narrow ledge where the bit of gorse-bush grew. I swung my feet over, crouched and quickly straightened. I had a terrible fear that it would suddenly blow away before my hands closed over it.

I moved too quickly and grabbed too eagerly. As I freed the lace from the thorn, the cliff suddenly shivered under my feet. It was as if the handkerchief was a tacking thread. Pull the knot and everything fell to pieces. My feet vibrated. I felt dizzy. Sick. I swayed, lost my balance, grabbed at the gorse-bush. From under my feet, stones and pebbles went hurtling down. The cliff became a funnel. I heard the rattle of the pebbles magnified so that it seemed an avalanche was going on all around me. Still clutching the handkerchief, I covered my head with my hands. Pebbles spattered on my face.

I shouted as loud as I could, clinging to the cliff side. I don't know for how long. I tried to make my voice sound above the magnified rattle of the stones. A dry rocky dust, kicked up by the stones, half choked me.

And then I heard a voice.

At first I thought it was a humming in my ears, a sound mirage. But peering upwards, I saw a row of heads along the cliff top.

Then one in the centre acquired a face and neck and shoulders. Two distinct words: 'Hang on.'

I gulped.

I heard excited juvenile voices in the background. A family maybe on an outing.

The voice again. 'Don't worry. You're all right there. Bit of a rock fall. It's eased off, though.'

I didn't look to see. I kept my eyes on his face.

'That's it! Keep looking up! Don't look down!'

More excited twitterings in unbroken voices.

'Quick, Rob! Mister's found a bird on t'ledge. A real un, dope!'

The head and shoulders now were perilously extended. Brown hair haloed light in the sun, a calm pleasant voice quietly talking. 'My boys! Don't take too much notice of *them*. We'll have you up in a moment. We're experts at this sort of thing.'

A flash of white in the brown face above – a cue for me to smile. I managed a faint imitation.

'Cliff sides are beastly things. I remember once . . .' the quiet voice went on persuasively. He might have been coaxing a would-be suicide into safety. Then a whispered consultation.

'All right then, Rob. Take your time . . . but don't miss!'

A moment's silence. Then uncoiling dark against the blue sky came a rope with a loop in it to land neatly around my shoulders.

'Hey, whar-about-that-then?'

A cheer from the cliff top.

'Hey, mister, does Rob get a goldfish, then?'

Giggles – wonderfully reassuring. Now the persuasive voice again. 'Can you take hold of the rope? Good! Slip it under your arms. I'm going to pull a bit tighter. That comfortable?'

'Yes.' I got the single syllable out and nodded.

'Good girl! Right then! Up we come!'

I felt the pressure build up under my arms.

A boy's voice began singing 'The Volga Boatmen'.

The brown-haired man spoke again. 'Keep looking up at me. Don't look down!' A muscular arm reaching down the rope. A dark frieze of little boys' heads behind him. 'We're going to pull you up! There's a sheer cliff edge just above you. Keep it away with the flat of your hand.'

In mid-air I dangled. I could just see the pull of his arms, the swell of his muscles. The boys had disappeared, but I could still hear their voices.

The lichened grey granite moved downwards. I swayed, steadied myself with my hands and the sides of my feet. Then the two arms came down, caught me, and pulled me over the top.

'Not so bad, was it?'

'S'better than going the other way.' A tall thin bespectacled boy pointed to the rocks below. 'Ain't it, miss?'

I nodded, shuddered without effort.

The man helped me to my feet. 'Feel all right?'

'Fine now, thank you.' I began to feel foolish standing there with the rope still hanging round me like a lasso, and my hands still held in his. Seeing me glance down, he dropped them, began to untangle me from the rope.

'It was a stout effort. I don't know what I'd have done without you,' I said, murmuring my thanks to the circle of faces. Five of them, around ten to fourteen, all smiling back at me, shyly, proprietorially. I might have been some outsize fish they'd landed. So I was really. 'It was a good thing you saw me.'

The smiles widened. Hopefully from the bespectacled boy. 'Would you 'ave fallen, miss?'

I nodded vigorously. 'Any moment.'

'Or been hit by falling rocks?' The bespectacled boy again.

A rustle in the circle. A slender orange-haired boy of ten with one of those beautifully shaped heads on a spring onion neck Piero della Francesca used to paint was thrust forward to take a bow. The bespectacled youth kept his hand on his shoulder as if gluing him in the limelight. The little boy wriggled irritably. He had a slightly undershot jaw, large haphazard teeth that were too big for it. They rested on his lower lip and were gathered in at intervals noisily and spittily. 'Braddon here was look-out.'

'I'm jolly glad you've got sharp eyes, Braddon.' Unnerved by Braddon's pale blue protuberant stare, I watched the man's strong fingers rolling the rope, exchanged a grin with him at my auntyish tone. 'It's an unusual name, isn't it?'

'Sorry, I should have introduced you.' The brown-haired man turned. 'The Brothers Karamazov.' Laughs from the tall bespectacled boy and a slightly smaller replica without glasses, and frugally from Braddon. 'Otherwise known by their mother as Rob, Bill and Braddon Wilkins.'

'I got sharp ears too, miss.' Braddon moved a little closer.

'Brad the Ad,' the salesman brother said. ' 'Ears like an adder.'

The brown-haired man smiled. 'The farmer christened him that.' He moved down the circle. 'Next to Bill is Chick Harvey. Always peckish. And last but not least, Johnny McIntyre.'

'Scots?'

'Good heavens, no! Cockney like the rest.' The brown-haired man smiled shyly. 'As I am.'

'Whereabouts?'

'Oh, I don't live in London now. But I was born in Hampstead.' A pause. Another smile, a brown square hand extended, a firm warm grip. 'My name's Wayne.'

'Mine's Browning.'

'Bryan Wayne.'

'Olivia Browning.'

'Bryan with a Y.'

'Livvy for short.'

We both laughed. He had an attractive laugh – unhurried, unforced.

'We was on safari, miss, when suddenly –' Braddon apparently now desirous of the limelight insinuated himself between us – 'I heard the noise of falling rocks and this terrible scream.'

Bryan Wayne winked at me. I winked back, said nothing.

'Brad here was walking right at the edge . . .' The other brothers joined in, graphically explaining with added detail the events leading up to my rescue.

'What you need now, miss,' Rob Wilkins said, 'is a warm

sweet drink. Coffee or tea. That right for shock, mister?'

'Absolutely!' And to me, 'You've made their day.' The bunch of boys began to move away from the headland towards a rough path between the gorse and bracken. 'And now I fear you're going to be borne off to camp HQ like a captive mermaid.' He hesitated, flushed slightly. 'If you don't mind, that is.'

'I don't mind. I'm looking forward to that warm sweet coffee or tea.'

'You won't know the difference. I never do.'

'Shape of the pot,' I said. 'Tall for coffee, wide for tea.'

'Same billycan for both.'

The ground here was soft and springy. For a hundred yards we walked along in silence going east, away from Trethyddion. Then he said, 'Is it your hobby?'

'What?'

'Scaling cliffs.'

I laughed. 'Good heavens, no! It was just – ' I looked down at the crumpled white ball in my right hand, grubby with the grit from the dead diver's face – 'I'd lost my handkerchief.'

'Of sentimental value, no doubt?'

'Of value to me anyway.'

'At the risk of appearing stuffy – ' he was smiling at me – 'could I suggest you don't risk your pretty neck again for it?' And then, without any more questions, almost apologetically, 'It's another mile, I'm afraid.'

'What is?'

'Our camp.' The smile deepened. 'On the cliff top. You see, some of our chaps have never seen the sea.'

'Where do they come from?'

'They're Walworth boys.'

'Scouts?'

He shook his head vigorously. 'Nothing so respectable. They'd be drummed out. Real young toughs. As if you haven't noticed!'

'D'you bring them down for a holiday?'

'Oh, don't put me amongst the do-gooders! *I* come for my holiday. They come with me.'

'I'm on holiday too. Just arrived last night. But I lived here as a child. Is this your first time here?'

'Theirs, not mine. I try to bring a fresh lot for a month each summer. The boys seem to like this place. We have a whale of a time. Trekking, signalling, climbing, sailing, scuba-diving. We've got a boat on the beach. All the things they can't do at home.'

'They must love it.'

'*I* love it. Wouldn't do it otherwise. For eleven months of the year my life's so ordinary.'

'What do you do?'

'Three guesses.'

'You could be almost anything.'

'Nice of you. Guess just the same.'

I glanced at the brown muscular hands.

'The Army?'

'God, no.'

High forehead, narrow clever face, fluid expression, but ordinary, he had said. 'A clergyman?'

Outraged laughter. 'No marks whatsoever.'

'A solicitor?'

'Dear girl, quite cold!'

'What then?'

'Dullest of all. I teach science to the Sixth Form of a very expensive public school.'

I must have looked doubtful for he asked, 'You think this is a busman's holiday?'

I shook my head.

'These boys are so different. From my spoiled brats, I mean. More imagination. Inventive genii, some of them. Unconscionable liars too, naturally. Anyway – ' he smiled – 'it all balances out very satisfactorily.' Then, 'What do you do? Anything?'

For the next ten minutes, as we threaded our way through the heather and the bracken, we discussed our jobs, our lives, our views. We established various common factors – both lived alone, both unmarried, both without near relatives, both liked art and music.

'Do you paint?'

I shook my head. 'Not in the proper sense. I wish I did. Restoring isn't the same. I wish I could *capture* . . .'

I waved my hand. We were coming up to the camp now, where our arrival had been heralded by the advance group. Against the cliff and the horizon of the sea, were six white bell tents in a circle round a flagpole on which there fluttered the Union Jack. A trail of smoke, the same colour as the granite of the cliff, rose up from an iron barbecue. Round a bucket, three boys in shirt-sleeves sat peeling potatoes, while above them, whiter than the tents, great gulls circled, waiting. Simple, balanced, momentous.

'Photos aren't the same,' Bryan Wayne said, interpreting my thoughts.

Then wiping out the scene, flurrying it like wind over water, a gathering sound of motors. The gulls flew off. The boys looked up. Others appeared from the tents. Two helicopters swept southward, hovering low, bending the branches of the trees, rippling the grass.

'Navy choppers.' A boy by the barbecue aimed a poker like a gun. 'Bang, bang, bang!'

I clapped my hands over my ears. 'What on earth do all these helicopters do?'

Mr Wayne shook his head. 'God knows. What do any of these Service chaps do? The boys don't mind them, of course. They've got hold of some crazy story.' He laughed. 'You know the way they pick up the wrong end of the stick.'

'No, we don't, mister!' The orange-haired boy had come sidling up again. He insinuated himself between us, stared up at me compellingly. 'It's true, miss. Straight up!'

'Brad heard the story in the first place.' Bryan Wayne gave him a playful cuff on the side of his head.

'You know me, mister.' Whining slightly now.

'I do indeed, Brad. And I know when to take you with a pinch of salt.'

We had reached the barbecue. Sure enough a dark blue enamel billycan bubbled on the griddle. 'Coffee,' I said, sniffing. 'Unmistakable!'

'Tea.' Rob Wilkins sadly handed me an enamel mug. We all laughed.

Braddon came up and dropped in two lumps of sugar. He pointed to the helicopters now hovering lazily beyond the headland. 'They've lost sumfing, miss.'

'Damn Walworth cinema and their James Bond bonanzas!' Bryan said good-humouredly.

'Know where they're searching, miss?'

'Haven't a clue.'

'Round the wrecks. They think whatever it is is stuck on one of 'em.' He nodded the large head several times. 'People 'ave seen divers.' He flapped his hands and feet graphically.

Bryan was lighting his pipe. He snapped the lighter off, and dropped it in his pocket. 'It could have been some of your mates scuba-diving.'

'No. Straight up! Real professional.'

I must have drawn my breath in sharply, for Bryan Wayne said crisply, 'Now you've really frightened Miss Browning. Off with you, Braddon!' He looked at me with real concern and apology. 'No more of your nonsense!'

I felt I had to say something in Braddon's defence. 'I don't think it's necessarily nonsense.'

'Kind as well as beautiful,' Mr Wayne drained his mug. 'She'll even say that tea tastes delicious.'

'So it does.'

I watched the helicopters move a few hundred yards further away, hover at even height. The picture was forming up again. The boys on kitchen fatigues had resumed their chores. I heard the thud of peeled potatoes being flung into the bucket. Bryan Wayne was busy showing McIntyre how to gut a fish. Maybe the gulls could smell it, I thought, listening to them screaming overhead.

'Mind if I stroll round?' I tried to reassemble myself again, forget the past hours, as I had almost succeeded in doing.

Mr Wayne seemed pleased. 'Oh, do, yes!'

I stepped over the guy ropes, peeped inside one of the tents. After the sunshine a green gloaming like the shallows of the sea, the smell of crushed grass, rubber groundsheets, toothpaste, canvas. Everything made neat, blankets folded stacked, clothes on hangers hooked to the tentpole.

'Psst, miss!' An urgent, spitty whisper, an upraised warning finger over the toothy O of the small mouth. 'Over here!'

At the far end of the tent, the glow of orange hair. The upraised hand beckoning urgently. Braddon stooping down under the blankets digging conspiratorially. I let the flap fall behind me, moved forward, oddly compelled by the child's vehemence

He straightened. He had something cupped in his hands, hidden by his fingers.

'You won't breathe a word, miss?'

'No.'

'Not to anybody.'

I shook my head. 'I promise.'

'Cross your heart and hope to die.'

Entering, it seemed, into yet another conspiracy, I crossed my heart.

'Say it.'

I said it.

Like a large pink oyster shell, the cupped hands began to open. The greeny gloom of the tent, the shadow of the upper hand – something there, difficult to see, a silky sheen to it, a curved piece of jagged metal, about three inches long.

'It,' he whispered.

I didn't know what he meant.

'It,' he repeated. 'IT,' emphasizing the one word, louder as if to drill it into my thick skull.

'What?'

'It. What they lost.'

'Isn't it rather small?'

'Oh, this here's just a bit, miss. But a bit of *it*.'

'Where did you find it?'

'Under the sea.'

'In Trethyddion Bay?'

'Ah. That'd be telling! Then you'd know as much as me.' Abruptly the oyster shell closed. A quick movement like a conjurer in reverse, lightning sleight of hand, the flap of a blanket, abracadabra. It had disappeared.

Brad stood up straight. All was over. We emerged from the green twilight into the sunshine. I half expected him to ask me to cross his palm with silver.

'What've you two been up to?'

'Nothing, mister.'

'Brad the Ad chatting up our bird.' McIntyre was still struggling with the backbone of the fish. Bryan Wayne was washing his hands in a tin bowl. 'Have another cuppa?'

'No, thanks. I really must be going.'

'Stay for supper.'

'High tea'll be waiting for me. Mrs Luxford will be getting worried again.'

'Mrs Luxford?'

'Where I'm staying. At the coastguard cottage. The one on Trethyddion Head. You can't miss it.'

'Oh, yes, I know it. All white walls and shutters. But you're not the girl who lives there?' He looked astonished. 'Works at the White Horse?'

'You mean Vasha. Do you know her?'

'I've had a drink at the pub. Been there yet?'

'No.'

'Nice place. Let me take you one evening.'

'I'd like that.' I looked at my watch. 'And now I must fly.' I shouted my goodbyes and thanks to the boys. They waved back. Bryan and I began walking across the camp field, while from behind us came the intermittent beam and click of an Aldis lamp.

'Brad the Ad signalling.'

'What's he saying?'

Bryan turned, shielded his eyes. His lips moved. He smiled. 'Will ye no' come back again?'

I was quite overcome.

'That goes for all of us.' Bryan touched my arm. 'Especially me.'

'Thank you.'

'And will you?'

'I'd like to.'

Silence for a few steps. 'I've got my car over there.' He indicated a white Lotus. 'Though I must say selfishly, I'd rather walk.' He gave me an engaging sideways smile. 'But if your landlady will be worried . . .'

We went by Lotus – quickly and efficiently. At Mrs Luxford's front door, I said, 'That story the boys have got hold of . . . it *is* possible, you know.'

Bryan laughed. 'Of course it's possible. But I'm a scientist, you know. Given to theorems and formulae and scientific certainties. Blood and thunder aren't my cup of tea.'

He smiled and squeezed my hand as he walked with me up the path.

'Don't forget your promise.'

'My promise?'

'You've forgotten already!' He looked at me quizzically. 'To come back again.'

'I'd love to.'

I paused just before we reached the cottage. I didn't want to take him inside to Mrs Luxford's questioning and fussing.

Besides, it seemed we had a visitor. There was a smart blue van parked beside the cottage, half hidden by the bushes of the lane. It had the letters ROYAL NAVY picked out in white.

Vasha's voice through the open window announced, 'Here she comes now.'

The billowing curtains were pulled aside. A man's face, a big out-thrust jaw and mouth crammed with food, stared out at me. Vasha calling, 'Weelyum, manners please.' So this was William.

I walked up the path. The front door was already open. William pulled it further back. He towered above me. He was big-boned, broad-shouldered, tough-looking, wearing a brown checked shirt, sleeves rolled up, open at the neck showing a V of hairy chest. For all the youthful clothes – studded leather belt with camping knife and holder, tight jeans – about thirty-five. Incongruously, Mrs Luxford's lace-edged napkin tucked inside his leather belt.

'There's not much left, love. But come on in.' A hand outstretched, 'I'm Mr Hardaker. William. Pleased to meet you.'

He had a faint Midlands accent, a crushing handclasp. He rushed forward to pull out a chair for me. He moved with exaggerated looseness like a jointed puppet. Even then I remember thinking, 'Who pulls the string?'

'I hope you didn't mind us starting, Livvy?' Mrs Luxford rose, glanced at the clock. Almost half-past five.

'I was starving,' William slapped his stomach, slid back into his chair, stuffed a forkful of ham and salad into his mouth.

'You were ever such a long time, m'dear.' Mrs Luxford set a plateful of ham in my place. I went through into the kitchen to wash my hands. I smoothed my hair. I heard William whisper hoarsely, 'Yus. Very pale. Thin an' all.' I was clearly not his cup of tea.

'We couldn't wait for the crabmeat,' William said. 'Had to make do with the ham.'

'Sorry, I forgot all about it. I walked further than I meant to.'

'Get to Port Navar at all, did you, m'dear?'

I shook my head. I helped myself to salad, filled my mouth as if I were ravenous. When I opened it again, the crabmeat and Port Navar were forgotten. I asked Vasha if she had been busy at the White Horse.

'Hardly a soul.'

'There's a good reason for that.' William picked his teeth.

'Is there, Mr Hardaker? And what might that be?' Mrs Luxford replenished William's plate.

'Well, keep it within these four walls.' He lowered his voice. 'There's a Red One Alert. Up at you-know-where.'

'Weelyum, Weelyum!'

William ignored Vasha. He turned to me. 'Know what that means, Ollie?'

'No.'

'It means all personnel to report for duty. And it means Herr Commandant Captain is up you-know-what creek without a paddle.'

'Why?' I said, as he seemed to expect something from me.

'You shouldn't ask that.' He was obviously pleased I had done so. 'Hush-hush. But between friends – ' he lowered his voice again – 'they've lost an ASD. That to the ignorant – ' he looked at me – 'is an anti-submarine device. And brother, they gotta find it! Or heads will roll!'

'Not *yours*, I hope, Mr Hardaker?'

'Not mine, no, Mrs Luxford. I just get on wiv me work and do what I'm told.'

'What exactly *do* you do?' I asked.

'There she goes again! Proper little nosey parker, isn't she? Well, I'll tell you, Ollie! I drive these perishing boffins hither an' yon. I drive their silly little devices hither an' yon. I drive the crew of the HSL's. Those, to the ignorant, are High Speed Launches. I change the watches on the OP's.'

'What are those to the ignorant?' I asked.

'Observation posts. Where they have the theodolytes. Those to the ignorant – '

'I know what those are,' I said. 'They measure angles.'

'But not today, brother. No position fixing. No frying tonight! Nothing. Our little device has been and gone and scarpered into the high blue yonder. *And* it's an operational one, not a practice.' He handed up his plate to Mrs Luxford and she put on another slice of ham. 'Defected, I shouldn't wonder.'

He jerked his thumb over his shoulder. 'Know what's out there, Ollie?'

'The sea.'

'And what's on the sea?'

'Ships.'

'What sort of ships?'

'Trawlers mostly.'

'Doing what?'

'Fishing.'

'Aye, aye. But not for fish.' He leaned over the table. 'Those are Russian trawlers out there.'

He paused.

'He tells no lie,' Mrs Luxford said. 'Come right in if the weather blows nasty.'

'They got every sort of gubbins on 'em that you care to name, Ollie. More gadgets than Mrs Luxford's kitchen. Listening apparatus. Tracking stuff. Radar. They pick every radio impulse that anything along here sends out.'

I glanced at Vasha. She rolled her eyes and smiled.

'Oh, you cats may grin. Other people take them trawlers very seriously.'

'I'm sure they do, Weelyum.' She squealed good-humouredly.

He gave her a spiteful little kick under the table. 'Did you know that our Herr Commandant Captain gets a daily report on exactly where those bastards are? They're plotted in the Ops Room. I've seen it with my own blue eyes.'

'How come you got in there, Weelyum?'

'Picking up the duty officer, if you must know. I tell you it made my short and curly curlier. Those Russians don't miss a trick.'

'Ah, no. There I disagree, Weelyum. The Russians are stupid. Cruel, yes, ruthless, yes. But stupid.'

'She hates 'em, does Vasha,' Weelyum said to me approvingly.

'With good reason,' I said.

'They watch all our exercises,' William went on, not to be diverted. 'And for why, Ollie?'

'I suppose they want to find out our secrets.'

'You bet your sweet life they do! To protect their nuclear submarines.'

'I've read about those.'

'So you know everything about them, Ollie? You *know* that they never need to surface. You *know* their underwater speed is faster'n any aircraft carrier. You *know* that each one of them carries sixteen atomic rockets that would wipe out the West. You *know* that their propellers are shielded so they don't make no noise, so the old ASD's are so much scrap for Steptoe and Son.'

Vasha shook her head but went on fondly stroking his hand. 'Take no notice of him, Olivia.'

'And you, Ollie, as flippin' First Lord of the Admiralty, you *know* all this. You've spent your Saturday sixpence cooking up a nice little bottle of pop that'll make those Russian submariners – '

'Weelyum, *language* . . .'

'And you get your boffin scientists to make a torpedo, carrying thermoneuk punch if need be. But no bigger'n a codling, so it can be dropped by parachute. Softly, softly. And then the salt water starts up its engine. And you've put a special homing device on it. And you've made a special target so you could do trials on it. And you've christened it Scorpio and you've given it for Christmas to Herr Commandant Captain at you-know-where. And *then* what happens, Ollie?'

I shook my head. 'I don't know.'

'Come early yesterday morning, Herr Commandant Captain wants to play with it. Helicopters, HSL's, OP's . . . all manned. But it's windy, Ollie, sea's choppy . . . and as I drive him down to the harbour, I politely point this out to Herr Commandant Captain. And Herr Commandant Captain says to me, Hardaker, you bloody – '

'Weelyum, *language* . . .'

'So the helicopter drops. But the Russian trawlers have been listening on the radio, and under cover of the weather, in they come and do all sorts of nasty things. And as a result, you, Ollie, as flippin' First Lord of the Admiralty, have lost your Little Lamb. And if I was you, Ollie, I'd give Herr Commandant Captain a shot up his – '

'Weelyum, *language* . . .'

' – back rudder.'

'So the Russians have got Scorpio, Weelyum?'

'Might have.' He put his finger to one side of his nose. 'Might not have. But I don't think so. And for why? There were six trawlers there Thursday morning, and there are still six. If you was Comrade Admiral, Ollie, and you'd got Herr Commandant Captain's tingaling, you'd want to go home to play with it, now wouldn't you? Stands to reason. And as a result, everybody's playing Hunt the Thimble . . . Russkies, helicopters, HSL's, agents, Navy, Herr Commandant Captain – ' William stood up and put his hands stiffly to attention by his side – 'and Uncle Tom Cobleigh Hardaker and all.'

'So shall I not see you this evening, Weelyum?'

'Depends,' he said mysteriously, taking hold of her arm. 'You, girl, have got to learn to keep a stiff upper lip.' He twisted her arm behind her back in a half nelson, smiled as she squealed. 'If you're going to be a sort of Navy wife.' He released her arm. 'Well, Mrs Luxford, thanks for the nosh. 'Fraid it's time to love you all and leave you. Kiss you, Vasha, though, this time.'

He pulled her to her feet. A big embrace was imminent.

Then the telephone rang. Vasha released herself with surprising alacrity. She ran upstairs.

She came quickly back down again. 'It is for you, Livvy. A man.'

William made some ribald remark as I went upstairs. For some reason I was sure it would be the police or Curtis. The diver would have been found. The mystery about to be cleared. I lifted the receiver, said cautiously, 'Hello.'

Bryan Wayne's genial voice came back to me. 'So that, I suppose, was Vasha. What a charming voice. I hope you don't mind my phoning. I took the liberty of getting your landlady's number out of the book. You see we didn't make an actual date to continue our conversation.'

I was still vaguely disappointed it was Bryan. But we made a date for the following evening at seven-thirty. I heard Vasha come running lightly upstairs as I put down the receiver.

'So what do you think of my little Weelyum?' Vasha called to me gaily as I went by the open bathroom door. She was washing herself. Her reflection in the medicine cupboard window smiled at mine.

I was at a loss for words. 'He's quite a dish.'

'I thought for surely you would like him. He is big and handsome too, is he not?'

'Very.'

'And you think that we are suited? That we make a good pair?' She waved me to come and have a girlish chat. She was all coy smiles and blushes. Different from this morning. A Joseph's-coat-of-many-colours girl. Acting her part well.

I took a couple of steps into the bathroom. There is hardly room enough for one. I sat myself on the edge of the bath. 'I am very happy,' Vasha said. Her smile was sweet and unfeignedly friendly. 'And I am very happy for you too.'

'For me?' I looked surprised.

'You too have made a good-looking gentleman friend, have you not?'

'D'you mean – ' I gestured towards Mrs Luxford's room and the telephone – 'him?'

'Your caller. Yes. He has a very good-looking voice.' She laughed at the expression on my face. 'Oh, one can tell, I assure you. *I* can.' She reached for a towel, dabbed her face, glanced at me archly from between the towel's folds. 'He is handsome, isn't he?'

'In a way.'

'Is he tall? What colour is his hair? His eyes. Describe him to me.'

She listened to my description with an air of rapt romantic interest. Brows raised, lipstick held in mid-air. Pale mouth forming an exaggerated O.

'You see, I am right. He sounds very handsome. Just the man for you, Livvy. Refined, is that the word? What is his name?'

'Bryan Wayne.'

She said it over several times, rolling it round her tongue for taste. Then she said, 'Olivia Wayne.'

'Steady on.'

'No, I think it is attractive. I like it. It is nearly as sweet on the tongue as Vasha Hardaker.'

'Nothing could be as good as that,' I smiled.

'And how did you manage to meet him so quickly?' She began to outline her lips. 'Handsome men do not fall from the skies. Even for you, Livvy.'

I explained about my search, the spotting of the handkerchief on the cliff side.

She laughed. 'And then, *he* came along, this Mr Wayne, and climbed it for you. Livvy, that is a very old trick. The dropped hankie. I am surprised at you.'

'Not quite. I climbed up myself.' I told her about the rock fall and the rescue. 'And don't say that I did that deliberately too.'

She laughed teasingly. 'I have not heard of many rock falls down here.'

'I have. Especially after a wet summer.'

'Then it was a very dangerous thing to do.' She shook her head reprovingly, unscrewed a little bottle of lash glue and fixed back one false lash. 'Was it really so important?' She fixed the other. 'That hankie?'

'Of course it was. Don't you see? It's proof that I was down there!'

She turned her head, blinking. 'To whom, Livvy?'

'To me.'

'Shall you take it to the police?'

'Of course not. What good would that do? They'd just laugh. Or think I was mad.'

She nodded, absorbed now in painting the big black sweeps on her eyelids.

'I hope you threw it away, then.'

'No, I didn't.'

I put my hand in my pocket and brought out the crumpled handkerchief. I held it towards her. The effect on her was electric.

'I don't want to touch it. Take it away!'

Granted, the smell of it was slightly unpleasant, but her reaction was exaggerated. She dropped her eye shadow. Threw up her hands. Made a face of loathing distaste.

'Oh, Livvy! How could you? It has his spittle on it. The dead man's. Throw it away! Please! It is unhealthy! Unlucky too to carry round what has touched the dead!'

She pointed dramatically to Mrs Luxford's floral wastepaper basket. 'It has proved its point. You have no further use for it.'

She seemed now to be in genuine distress about it. Suddenly showing up the superstitious side of her Slavonic nature, I remember thinking. I did as she urged me. She was right. It had proved its point. To me, anyway.

I tossed it into the bin.

Immediately, she covered the offensive scrap of material from our sight with a handful of Kleenex tissues.

There was another errand to do that day. I told Mrs Luxford I had a card to post to the people at the Bullingham, and this time I'd take the car and I really wouldn't be gone long. I left her sitting in front of the television watching *The Generation Game*. If William were right, that momentous event would be plotted aboard one of the distant Russian trawlers, and its significance pondered at international level.

And though I discounted ninety per cent of what he said, I didn't discount all.

I let myself out of the cottage and turned the Triumph round. It was dusk outside now, and cold. There was a soft pink afterglow in the west, the colour and texture of fondant.

I drove down the lane with my sidelights on, and turned on to the main highway. The traffic was light. The main press of nine-to-five workers in St Edzell's and Pendragon already gone home, and the evening-outers were not yet on the road.

I drove west for a couple of miles, then pulled the car to one side opposite the illuminated rectangle of the telephone-box.

I got out and crossed over.

There were no signs of damage inside the box. No sign of Curtis's vandals. In the mirror over the instrument I caught sight of my own face. It seemed to have changed in the last twenty-four hours. I looked pale, as William had said. A frown line had appeared between my brows, marring my usually smooth forehead, giving me an unaccustomed distracted look.

I lifted the mouthpiece. I heard the dialling tone.

That was still not complete proof that the telephone was working. I dialled 999 and waited.

'Emergency. What service?'

'Police, please.'

Almost immediately the line clicked open the other end. The sergeant's voice answered. 'St Edzell police. Yes? Who's calling?'

I hesitated, almost hung up, I should have done. Left them to assume it was some joker.

'Where are you calling from? Speak up.'

'This is Olivia Browning.' Immediately I could feel the chill.

I hesitated. The sergeant's voice cut in coldly. 'Is it an emergency? You've come through emergency, miss. Did you know? Have you found . . .' His voice broke off as if he'd covered the mouthpiece.

'I was ringing,' I said, 'to see if you've any news?'

'Of what, miss?'

'Of the diver. Has he turned up?'

A long pause. 'No, miss. The diver hasn't turned up.'

'Has anyone been reported missing?'

Another pause. A subtle change of tone. Friendly almost. 'There's always people reported missing. Specially down here, this time of year. Go for a holiday. Don't come home. But they're usually all right.'

'Anyone who fits the description?'

'Your description? No, miss.'

I thanked him and hung up.

After that, to make sure the box was working for ordinary calls too, I looked up the number of the only place apart from Mrs Luxford's that I could think of, the White Horse in St Edzell's. I got through without difficulty. I asked them how late they served supper snacks. A voice that sounded like Vasha's answered, but she didn't seem to recognize mine.

I walked slowly out of the box and back to the car.

So Curtis had got through to someone last night, had obviously told them about the body on the beach.

Was it the police? Or someone else? And why?

I got into the Triumph and started it thoughtfully. Who was Curtis? Where did he come from? What, besides a liar, was he?

Heavy feet on the stairs.

Another nightmare – that was my first waking thought. The old recurring horror dream of childhood. Nothing but one's own heartbeat, the nervous blood pounding in the pillow-pressed ear. No crack of light showed under my bedroom door. The house was shut up.

The steps paused.

My heart went on pumping. Above the shelter of the sheet, my eyes rolled to the little phosphorescent ticks of the bedside clock.

Three-thirty.

Before going to bed, Mrs Luxford and I had talked. Deliberately, it seemed to me, she had avoided the subject of the dead diver. She had handed me Mr Luxford's photograph taken in front of the old Wheal Fortune stamping house. She had brought out others, tried to take me back to happier times. She had found one of me aged seven taken in front of the big whim. Odd how photos bring it all back! As she had intended. I said I remembered the trips Mr Luxford and I used to make down the mines. And I reminded her of my father's patent invention, a machine for testing for ore which was never built.

Mrs Luxford clicked her tongue and went on crocheting. 'Trouble with your Da, all his geese were swans.' She looked at me suddenly over the top of her spectacles. 'Like all your rocks are dead divers,' her monkey eyes said.

'He was ahead of his time. That's exactly what they're doing now. Reopening the mines.'

'Not that 'un. They won't open up Wheal Fortune.'

'Why? Because the sea's got into her?'

'Folk were never meant to tunnel under the water.'

I had a vivid recollection of Mr Luxford telling me before the submarine stopes were breached that when he was a boy, working on the sea bed stage, he used to hear the sound of the waves dragging the pebbles over his head.

'There are bounds to what folk should meddle in.' She gave me another meaningful look.

'Finding a dead man isn't meddling,' I said.

'I didn't say it was. I didn't mention it.'

I leaned forward. I spoke softly. 'That's just *it*. *Why* don't you mention it?'

She shrugged.

'It's true.'

She sighed. 'Then how could he get up and spirit himself away?'

'Someone *took* him away.'

'But *they'd* leave tracks. The sand'd be all smuttered up.'

'There was rain.'

'Even so.'

I touched her arm. 'Look at me.'

Reluctantly her eyes met mine.

'Was I ever a liar?'

Indignation. 'That you were not.'

'Well then?'

Real tears at that. Poor old girl. No wonder I had nightmares afterwards. She whipped off her glasses. Dabbed her eyes, polished her glasses, faced me again.

I went on. 'So you don't really think I made it all up? Deliberately?'

'That I don't.'

'And I didn't imagine it?'

Less surely. 'No.'

'Then *what*? There's nothing else. You must believe me.'

A quivering indrawn breath. 'There *is* something else, Livvy.'

'Then tell me what.'

Another long pause. 'Sometimes dead folk appear before they're rightly dead. To them that see. You ask any miner. Ask any real Cornish Jack. They'll tell you it's so. The gospel truth. Dead and dying come at the pick point of death. And them that see, sees.'

'A ghost! Are you telling me I saw a ghost?'

'A spirit about to meet its Maker,' she corrected. 'That is why he left no trace. That's why others couldn't see him.'

For all the warmth in that room, I had shivered.

Tired though I was, that theory had haunted me. I had lain awake for a long time turning over what she had said. The curtain undrawn, I had watched the headlamps of cars blossom and vanish along the highway, the steady false dawn of the Pendragon complex. I had heard Mrs Luxford put the milk bottles out at the back door and then come upstairs to bed. I had listened for the sound of the helicopters, and they had come. One after the other, the curious engine noise out of the tunnel of the night. One after another, the little cracked brooches of red and green and glass diamonds had glided across my window pane, drawn towards St Edzell's like magnets to metal. Then out over the coast, I suppose. Night exercises, Mrs Luxford said. Searching, according to William. But for what? And how, bat-like, by night?

I counted them like sheep, getting steadily more drowsy till Vasha came in, and then I must have fallen asleep.

Now this. I sat up in bed listening.

The steps had still stopped. I was imagining things. *Again*, the police would say. Everything was quiet. There was only the tinny ticking of the clock, the sound of a helicopter, lower than the rest, rattling the window-panes.

A creak. A creak on the stairs. Only the vibration from those engines, already the chopper sound was dying away.

Another creak – the old cottage settling down for the night. Walls cooling, wood contractiug. Scientific explanation.

Another creak. Why always on the stairs? My heart was pounding again. But the creaks had no rhythm, no sense to them.

There was only one more. Close – the topmost tread. A faint slight brushing noise. Breathing?

Someone paused outside my bedroom door.

I gripped the top of the sheet, bade myself throw back the covers, get out and look. Cowardice kept me sweating, paralysed, inert. Another helicopter flew over. Higher, only lightly shimmering the frames. Under the cover of its sound, I would have sworn a door opened and as softly shut.

Mine?

In the darkness, I couldn't be sure. Did the darkness of the room seem thicker over there? Did the wardrobe shelter another shape? Did a shadow solidify at the bottom of the bed?

My hand fumbled for the lamp switch. I half expected a Curtis grip on my wrist. Creaks, shadows, nightmares conjoined, swooping forward to disclose their three-dimensional menace.

The pink shaded light showed a harmless empty room. No dead diver. No intruder. No body. Me and my imaginings alone.

Could it, I shivered, have been an apparition?

Could it have conceivably been my imagination all along? I went over everything again, from other people's point of view. Curtis, the police, Mrs Luxford, Vasha, William. For all their varying expressions of belief and disbelief, what did they really think?

Steeped as Cornwall is in warnings of disaster, ghostly appearances, could I have picked up some inexplicable manifestation? Or was it *déjà vu*? Had I slipped through some crack in time? *Relived* something that had happened before? Or was about to happen? Or was it all imagination again? A lonely time, nostalgia, dwindling light, the atmosphere of Trethyddion Bay . . . ?

I switched off the lamp. Imagination, nightmares, ghosts – firmly I closed my eyes to all of them.

And then another noise. Not a creak, not a thud. Not even very loud. A human sound. Indefinable. A sort of desperate smothered cry.

I didn't bother with the lamp. I threw back the clothes, stumbled my way to the door. Snapped on the wall switch. Crossed the little landing. Threw open Vasha's door.

A spreading cone of light spotlighted her bed.

Observing, but not registering, still continuing like a decapitated hen, I tripped over a pair of boots, pressed the switch. Full floodlight now on Vasha's tumbled hair, pale face and neck and naked breasts – her eyes blinded, her mouth open and reproachful. William glanced over his shoulder, face scorched with light.

'Please.' Vasha kept her dignity, clutched a handful of sheet and pulled it up to her chin. 'What do you want?' And turning the tables: 'Is it another nightmare you have?'

'I thought . . .' I began backing away.

'The light!' She waved her hand imperiously, screwing up her eyes.

'I thought,' I went on, 'I heard a noise. Someone screamed.'

'A nightmare. She has nightmares.' She put a hand on William's brown shoulder, running her fingers down his spine. 'You will catch cold – ' she turned back to me, reproachful again – 'without a gown. You should take some tablets to make you sleep.'

'I'm sorry,' I said abjectly, and softly closed the door. A tiny giggle wafted behind me across the landing. I took a couple of Anadins out of my handbag and climbed back into bed.

All the same, I heard William go. An hour later, socked

feet only gently creaking the treads. I heard the pause at the bottom of the stairs while he put his boots on and the quiet shutting of the outside door behind him. He must have left his van well up the lane. I didn't hear the engine start. But a few minutes afterwards I saw headlights going fast down the road towards St Edzell's.

I slept indifferently after that and got up late. I slipped on slacks and shirt. It was a crisp day with a touch of autumn. Mrs Luxford was sweeping the back garden path. There was a smell of wood smoke. Vasha, Mrs Luxford said, had finished her breakfast and gone. Just as well, I thought. I didn't feel like facing her. No doubt I would have been the embarrassed one.

I ate my boiled egg, home-made bread and farm butter in perfect peace. I propped the local paper – the *Western Morning Mail* – against the marmalade pot.

A small item in the Stop Press News caught my eye: *The naked body of a man was found on the beach near Marazion. Foul play is not suspected.*

Saturday

My first action on reading that Stop Press item was to go through to the back garden and announce to Mrs Luxford that I was going to do some shopping in St Edzell's. Some sixth sense warned me to keep everything as normal as possible. I had got over my initial shock. Those printed words had followed rather too closely on Mrs Luxford's theorizing for my emotional comfort. For the first few stunned moments, I had almost accepted her idea. Then slowly common sense had rescued me. I had thought carefully. Marazion is a good ten miles west of St Edzell's, and therefore about thirteen from where I had found the body. I don't know much about winds and tides and currents, but I'd say that body had drifted against them all.

I knew what I was going to do. Though I was terrified, nauseated at the thought of doing it.

'Shopping, m'dear?' She looked up crestfallen from shovelling waste paper and dead plants on to her little bonfire. 'I thought you might stay home and give me a hand.'

I apologized. I tried to appear relaxed. I didn't hurry. I even offered her a lift. Though I knew she wouldn't accept, because once she's put her hand to the plough, as she calls it, she doesn't give up.

'No. I must get this old rubbish cleared, m'dear. Dustbin men only come upalong here once a two week. They don't like this old lane.'

We discussed the difficulty of turning their lorry, of the general disobligement these days of dustbin men. She wouldn't let me get away. I felt she was trying to keep me talking. Giving someone *time*. For what? It was more than likely she had glanced at the paper. Had she, I wondered, seen that Stop Press item?

The ways of dustbin men being exhausted, she warned me about shopping on Saturday in St Edzell's. People stacked like cordwood. Everyone seemed to do their marketing then. The fair opened all day today, and folk would come in for that. Couldn't whatever I wanted wait till Monday?

I said I needed to get something rather urgently from the chemist. Then I excused myself abruptly. I cleared away my breakfast things, washed the dishes and went upstairs. I went to my room first to get my handbag. I heard Mrs Luxford puffing upstairs. I heard the click of the bathroom door behind her. I waited impatiently for what seemed ages.

When I finally got into the bathroom, I found what I feared I would find. The little waste-paper bin empty. The handkerchief gone.

I went downstairs. The bonfire was burning merrily. Mrs Luxford had just tipped some more waste paper on to it. I lifted the dustbin lid. Empty.

'You looking for something, then, Livvy?' Mrs Luxford called.

'My hankie. I put it in the bathroom waste-bin by mistake.'

She clicked her tongue. She murmured about the carelessness of young girls. I couldn't see the expression of her eyes. 'Was it a specially good one, then?' She came towards me.

'Not really. But I liked it.'

'Have a look round the house then, m'dear. I'm sure I'd've spotted if there was a good hankie in the rubbish. It's such a waste. You might have forgotten where you put it, or dropped it somewhere else.'

'Yes, miss. We did just think you might come.'

The *we* was neither official nor royal. It was a simple plural. The sergeant was not alone. Silhouetted against the window light was another man with his back to me. He turned. Jim Curtis. He raised a hand and smiled.

I said, 'I didn't recognize you.'

The sergeant glanced at me. Recognition, the glance said, was not the lady's strong point.

'Do I look so different by daylight, Miss Browning?' Curtis came over and lifted the flap of the counter for me to come into the office proper. Close to, I noticed fine lines round the very dark blue eyes, thick short lashes. He was dressed this morning in a grey polo-necked sweater and jeans. He wore rubber-soled canvas shoes, salt-water-stained.

'No. It was just that I didn't expect to see you.'

Curtis nodded. 'So often we see what we *expect* to see.'

He smiled as if he had scored a point. I suppose he had.

The sergeant pulled forward a chair. Treating me this morning like an honoured guest. Or an invalid. Curtis brought up another chair, straddled it, arms folded over the back, faced me, smiling. But above the smile, his eyes were watchful, intent, alert. As if by holding my every move under those twin blue microscopes, he would somehow learn *something*.

For a moment, no one said a word. The sergeant returned to his interrupted work. I could hear the scratch of his pen, his wheezy breathing, the smack of his heavy hand on the blotting pad, the sigh as he closed whatever book he was writing in and turned to me. 'Yes, miss? And what can we do for you?'

He knew why I had come. But he was going to make me say it.

'I saw that piece in the paper.'

'Which piece, miss?'

'About the body they found. The naked one. It was in the *Western Morning Mail.*'

'That rag.' The sergeant sighed. The silver chain winked. 'The Cornish *News of the Globe.* You don't want to believe all what you read in the papers, miss.'

'Wasn't it true?'

'Yes and no. Fact and fancy. What we're always up against.'

'What was true? Was there a body?'

'Yes. A body was found. That's a fact. But naked, no. Newspaper laddie's fancy.'

My heartbeat quickened. 'Was he in a diving suit?'

'No, miss, no. That's your . . .' he broke off in mid-sentence.

'What was he wearing, then?'

Curtis put in swiftly, 'Cotton ducks, a dark blue sweater, white socks, blue rubber boots.'

A false note there. Just too much description.

'How long had he been in the water?'

'Difficult to say, miss, really.'

'Had he been dead long?'

'No, miss.'

'Yesterday?'

'No earlier, miss.'

'What did he look like?'

Curtis got up from his chair and resumed his position by the window, his back to me. 'Fortyish. Oval face, hazel eyes.'

'Brown hair?'

'Blackish.'

'Thick?'

'Thin.'

'A beard. A wispy beard?'

'Clean-shaven.'

'In other words . . .' embarrassment, disappointment, frustration, anger, shook my voice. I paused to steady it. 'Quite unlike the body I found.'

'Quite unlike your description – ' a careful weighty differentiation – 'of the body you *say* you found.'

The sergeant felt he had had the last word. He picked up his pen. There was a long silence. Deliberately I let it go on and on. 'How is it, Mr Curtis,' I said at last, 'that you know so much about *this* body?'

He spun round, apparently surprised. 'Didn't you understand? I thought you'd have realized. I found the poor chap. That's why I'm here. I brought him in.'

I, said the fly, I saw him die.

'Was he on the beach?'

'No.'

'Where?'

'About eighty yards off shore.'

'What were *you* doing?'

'As it happens, I was in a boat.'

'Looking for something?'

'Your missing diver?' An ironic shake of the head. 'No.'

Another silence. Curtis said with finality, 'So the circumstances of finding this body were different too.'

Out of their individual desire to get rid of me they both waited for me to get up and go. Curtis actually walked to the counter, put his hand on the flap. Ready to see me out like a perfect thankful gentleman.

I got up. Their faces brightened.

I paused. Their faces became impatient. I forced myself to say firmly, 'I would like to see the body.'

Odd that such a logical proposition should produce such immediate consternation in both of them. 'No, miss, no! We couldn't have that. Very public-spirited of you. But no need. Nasty old business. Very nasty.'

'You'd only upset yourself,' Curtis said coolly.

'Really, miss, I tell you. Your body and Mr Curtis's are quite different.'

'And into the newspaper immediately goes Mr Curtis's body. But mine, it's best to keep quiet about.'

The sergeant went a harassed hypertensive red. He looked genuinely bedevilled. A well-meaning man. But thick. Led, I remember thinking even then, by cleverer people.

He blustered, 'Now you look here, miss, you never did show us a body.' Mumbled about their attitude being for my own good. Finished off with once again, 'We can't rightly be sure there ever was one, now can we?'

'*I'm* sure.'

Silence again, and yet not silence. For though there was no sound audible to human ears, some sixth sense of mine felt the vibrations of their minds working. Some plan was being hatched. I was to be told something. Not the whole truth. Nor anything like a part of it. Just something, a verbal sedative, which would keep me quiet!

'She's obviously still worried.' Curtis said at last. He looked at the sergeant over my head. A speaking glance. 'Let her have a look, Sergeant. Don't suppose she'll settle till she does.' Slowly. '*Put her mind at rest.*'

The sergeant hesitated. Then shrugged, allowed himself to be overridden. Fool. Curtis walked to the door, taking the sergeant's acquiescence for granted.

'I'll just give them a tinkle.'

'There's a telephone in the charge room, sir.'

'Thanks.'

More scratchings of the sergeant's nib. More vibrations coming in on my mental radar, my female antennae. Telephones and Jim Curtis were a dubious combination in my mind. And why not use the telephone six inches from the sergeant's moving pen?

Curtis came back again. Kindly understanding smile, 'Well, that's fixed. I'll run you down. Though – ' he shrugged his shoulders – 'it's even more unnecessary now. He's been identified.'

A relieved smile in the sergeant's eyes. 'Has he, sir?'

'Yes, by his Captain.'

'Good. That helps to clear things up a bit.'

'Poor chap fell overboard.'

'From a trawler?' I asked.

Just a moment's hesitation. 'No, a coaster.'

'A *British* coaster?'

'A *French* one.'

His hand just lightly under my elbow. 'I've got my car parked on the front.'

'Mine's nearer.'

We were in the corridor out into the street.

'Parked the car round the side. Can't trust those bluebottles. Have you for parking while you're giving them a hand inside.'

The MG was all right – it hadn't disappeared. He unlocked the door, opened it for me, unlocked the steering wheel. Definitely not the trusting type.

Now we were actually going there, I was trembling again. I wished I hadn't insisted. Maybe, I began thinking to myself, I didn't see a body at all. Like a voice in a magnetizing tape I heard Curtis say, 'Not far luckily . . . thought it best to bring him here . . . they did a PM . . . drowning, of course . . . helluva lot of liquor inside the poor chap . . . Captain said there'd been a party.'

Then Curtis's face close to mine, looming suddenly concerned, *exaggeratedly* concerned. 'Look, should you? Don't! You'll only distress yourself. Leave well alone.'

And as he leaned over me, the certainty that he was lying, the therapeutic certainty. 'You're on holiday here. Relax. For God's sake stay out of this, until it's time to go home.'

Stay out of what?

'I'm all right. Just drive fast, that's all. I'd rather not talk.'

He slid over the cross-roads on the amber light. Past a multiple store, another amusement arcade. Past a market. Some holidaymakers with sweaters over their summer dresses. A fruit stall. Apples. Flowers. The smell of chrysanthemums. The car sliding in to the kerb.

'All right. Here now.' Taking my arm this time. Glass swing doors. A dark shadowy window. An enquiry desk. A face not unlike *his* behind the glass. God, was I seeing things? Curtis doing the talking. My arm again. Endless tiled corridors. Nightmare corridors. Never dwindling. Footsteps echoing back. White tiles now. A disinfectant smell. Very strong. Lysol. Behind Lysol a smell of damp earth. A door opening. Three-dimensional, icy cold. Whiteness. Cold lapping up like that cold from the cliff. The Lysol smell was not quite subjugating the smell of *death*. Soft words. The sound of a heavy door opening. Something running on metal runners. I closed my eyes. I opened them again. A quick lift of white.

The face snapped into shocked vision. Printed, photographed itself. I shook my head. The face wiped away under the white cover. Still in my mind, though.

'It's not him, is it?'

'No.'

'You're sure?'

'Yes.'

It was the key to be let out. Into the corridor. The Lysol smell fading behind us. Mr Curtis waved at the walrus face behind the glass. I felt the blow of cool air on my face. My stiff legs walked. I was inside the MG again.

'And now I'm going to buy you a drink.'

I couldn't speak. I just nodded. We rounded a cream row of Georgian houses on to the promenade. The sun struck a white dazzle from the sea, and then was doused in a shadowy yard in front of a big bow-windowed pub. A painted sign of a white horse hung above us.

It didn't even immediately penetrate that he had brought me to the pub where Vasha worked, because the trembling had started up again. It wasn't only shock at what I'd just seen. It was fear – fear of all the unknown things behind that awful impassive stone face that still floated in front of me. Certainly he had no beard; certainly he was clean-shaven. And then it came to me, he was *too* clean-shaven. Hair goes on growing after death. This face was smooth, shining smooth, alabaster smooth. This face had been closely shaved not long before we two arrived.

Curtis pushed open the saloon bar door. We were submerged in a beer-smelling gloaming. The room was dark, full of empty brown chairs arranged round brown tables. There was music from a juke-box in the corner, soft and sad. Opposite the door, a brass-canopied bar, all bright lights and bottles multiplied in peach-tinted mirrors. A bald-headed man in shirt-sleeves was drawing lager. Vasha was at the far end, arranging snacks on a white cloth.

I shivered.

'You'll feel better after a stiff drink.'

Curtis's fingers on my elbow tightened. I couldn't have pulled my arm away if I'd tried. We walked like that, close as lovers, towards the big lit stage of the bar.

'This is an unexpected pleasure.' Vasha wiped her hands, and glided towards us.

She raised her eyes from our togetherness and shot me a look of amused apology. Until then I had forgotten about last night. About Weelyum and her in bed together. Her look reminded me. What are you, it demanded, decadent swinging British, or prim English maid? Then something she saw in my face made her expression sharpen. She turned to Curtis.

'What may I get for you, sir?' Asked with custom-tailored charm. The verbal equivalent of her fingers down the lorry-driver's spine.

'Two double scotches and a pint of Worthington.'

He pulled out a stool for me and another for himself. But before he sat down, he went over to the juke-box, put in tenpence, made his selection. Out came an old 1930's song . . . *no more money in the bank, no cute baby here to spank, what's to do about it . . . ?* Then he came back to the counter. We sat so close, our thighs were touching. He pulled out a pipe from his pocket and asked me if I minded before lighting up. It was all cosy and courteous and natural and yet so fraught with undercurrents that were not, I swear, entirely mine.

'We'll have a bite to eat while we're here.' He looked at his watch. 'Do you good.'

I was too numb to argue. I wanted to escape him, but I

didn't know how. It wasn't just convention that bound me, though that came into it. It was as if I had no will-power or ingenuity left.

I listened to Curtis order a selection of sandwiches from Vasha. I watched her press the glasses against the upended whisky bottle. She stared at me as she did so in the tinted mirror. I saw my distress being noted. In a clinical way, without involvement. Not as a friend notices. But was she my friend? Did I trust her? Dare I go on confiding in her? Wasn't she all things to all men? A chameleon, changing for survival with the company she kept?

Had she really believed my story or only pretended to? If pretence, why? So that I would tell her more? Might it not be best to keep quiet?

I pressed my knees together to stop them shaking. I didn't want Curtis to know what a state I was in. My female antennae warned me against showing weakness to him. Though wasn't some sign of distress only natural? I'd seen two dead men in forty-eight hours. Or was it only one? Or none?

'And a Worthington for you, sir?'

Curtis nodded, slid both whiskies over to me. 'Let's see you drink those. *Both* of them. Come on. Down the hatch.'

My teeth rattled against the rim of the glass. He gave me a faint, deceptively sweet smile. Sad, almost. I wished I could trust him.

'Do you want soda or something in all that whisky, Livvy?'

I shook my head, gulped down some more.

'Livvy.' Curtis mulled over the name. 'Nice. Yes, I like it. Less touch-me-nottish than Olivia. Olivia is the lady in the gallery with the ikons and the zircons and the Modiglianis.'

A lucky shot that? A mere coincidence? Or a veiled

threat? The Bullingham had bought Modigliani's *Alice* last spring, at an extravagant price. It was reported in most of the papers. And I was the most junior member of the group that went to Beirut, the wicked city, to look at it.

Was Curtis trying to say he knew all about me? That he had ways and means of finding out?

'You make her sound like that statue, Galatea wasn't it, who had to be wakened with a kiss.'

'Olivia, perhaps,' Curtis said, 'but Livvy on the other hand is . . .'

'What?'

'More approachable. More adventurous. More . . .' he shrugged. 'May I call you Livvy?'

'If you want to.' Said stiffly, I know. But I couldn't help it. His conversation frightened me. I was out of my depth. For all his mantle of kindness Curtis was part of some conspiracy against me. I halted my thoughts there. Conspiracy. I was thinking in the jargon of the mentally disturbed. Getting a persecution complex.

'Yes, I do want to. And I'm Jim.' He clasped my hand as if we were meeting for the first time.

Vasha had been following these exchanges with a vague suspended smile, waiting to be introduced. 'Sorry, Vasha.' I said recovering myself. 'This is Jim Curtis. He gave me a lift on Thursday night. He was . . .' I hesitated. Finished conventionally, 'Very helpful.'

'Lucky I happened to be passing.'

'So fortunate for Livvy. Some people are not so kind.'

'I was glad to be of service.' A dry little smile.

'And I am very glad, Jeem, that she picked on you.' Vasha extended her hand over the counter.

'So am I.'

'Vasha lives where I'm staying. At Mrs Luxford's.' They

shook hands. One of them held on much longer than was necessary. I couldn't decide which. They both knew how to turn on the charm. They were both experienced exploiters of other people.

'Will you join us in a drink, Vasha?'

Vasha the chameleon chose a Babycham, the nice girl's drink. I watched her as she uncapped a bottle and poured it. She smiled ingenuously at Curtis, oblivious of the constant opening and shutting of the door, the cries for service. He seemed quite taken with her. I looked round for a way to escape. The Ladies was halfway down the room on the right. I wondered if there was a side exit through it to the street. When it got more crowded in here, could I gather myself together sufficiently to simply walk out?

He put his hand over mine again. 'Daydreaming, Livvy?'

'No. Just wondering.'

'Wondering what?'

'Where *you* live, Mr Curtis?'

'Jim, please.' He didn't answer me.

'I am afraid I took Livvy's favourite room. With the beautiful view.'

'I expect she'll survive.'

'She has been very sweet about it.'

'As one would expect.' A little dry smile covertly sarcastic. A pause, then, 'I expect she's glad of your company.'

'Oh, no. She is so good at finding her *own* company. Already, Jeem, since only Thursday evening. Already two . . .' she held up her fingers.

Two dead men, I thought. For all their smiles, maybe Vasha and Curtis thought that as well.

'. . . two handsome men.'

Curtis flicked a sharp sideways look at me. 'Who was the other chap you met?' he asked.

Vasha laughed. 'Ah, see, Jeem is jealous. Tell him, Livvy, how gallant Bryan was to you.'

I could see that the story of my cliff rescue was about to be repeated, so I said, 'He'd heard of you, Vasha. Where you worked, where you lived.'

Vasha seemed quite pleased. She dropped a cherry in her glass, stirred it round with a swizzle-stick, watched the bubbles burst with a little secret swallowed smile. 'Fame. That's what comes of being a barmaid.'

'A *pretty* barmaid.'

'Thank you, Jeem, and what do *you* do for a living?'

'I've been working abroad.'

'Doing what?' I asked.

'This and that.'

'And now?'

'I'm looking at a little sailing club and boatel that's up for auction.'

'Hence the boat?'

'Hence that.'

'So you might just settle here?'

'Might just.'

I lowered my voice. 'You didn't think it an inauspicious start? Finding *him*?'

He shrugged. 'These things happen.' A pause. 'To all of us.'

'Tell me,' Vasha put in gaily, breaking in on the manifest constraint between Curtis and me. 'Where have you two been this morning together? Somewhere nice?'

I caught my breath and Curtis said smoothly, 'We're somewhere nice *now*.'

'Yes, I think this place is nice. Homely.' Vasha waved at the bald-headed man, now continuously drawing beer as a steady stream of customers came into the bar. 'Everyone is so kind. And so are you, Jeem.' She raised her glass to Curtis. 'Cheers. Happy days! Is this for you two some sort of celebration?'

She smiled. Her bright squirrel eyes darted backwards and forwards from Curtis's face to mine.

'You *could* call it that, couldn't you, Livvy?' Curtis's hand rested affectionately on my arm.

'Could you?'

'Certainly.'

Further down the bar, a stout lady in a purple velvet hat drummed her fingers impatiently on the bar for service. Reluctantly Vasha left us to attend to her.

'We're celebrating,' Curtis said softly in my ear, 'the laying of a ghost.'

'That again.' Something that was happening somewhere else, or in the past, or was about to happen. A sensitive person tuning in to an emotional atmosphere, in the same way as those giant radar scanners tune in to sound. Mrs Luxford's theme. Rearranged with slightly different words, and set to different music. But the same. A conspiracy, no doubt of it. Now I didn't stop my own thoughts. But if a conspiracy, how many conspirators? Who were they? And what was their purpose?

I disguised my apprehension, and drank the whisky. I felt its molten heat coursing down inside me, doing its work. I smiled. 'I thought,' I said lightly, 'that ghosts had to be exorcized?'

'Sure.' Relief made Curtis unwary. He smiled back. 'Bell, book and candle.'

I watched Vasha serve a couple of men who looked like sailors. I drained the second glass, got the last drop of distilled courage. I turned to Curtis. 'How about soap, water, and razor?'

I turned quickly and caught the vivid flick of anger in his eyes. I saw the tightening of his jaw muscles before the bland mask came down. For minutes he said nothing. Vasha drifted back and put two plates of sandwiches in front of us. She glanced sharply at our faces, disappeared again. Neither of us touched the sandwiches.

Behind us the door opened and shut. The bar filled up. There was a murmur of voices all round, isolating us. Curtis gazed thoughtfully into his beer, swirled it around. Crystal-gazing.

'What made you say that?' he asked eventually in a conversational, even tone, his expression masked. He didn't look at me direct. He addressed my reflection in the peach-tinted mirror. And I answered his. It diluted us both somehow.

'Because the body I've just seen had been shaved.'

A long pause.

'A small matter of hygiene.'

'A small matter of making it unlike the one I found.'

Another long pause. Then dropping his voice still further, 'Livvy, listen to me.'

'I am listening.'

'That body on the beach did not exist. You *must* accept that.'

I spoke up angrily and loudly, 'But it does. That's the whole point. I know now it does.'

'Livvy, hush.' He put his arm round my shoulders as if comforting me. His face loomed over mine, eyes narrowed, lips thin and tight.

I tried to shake off his arm. 'I've been back. I found . . .'

The last words were smothered. In a quick pouncing movement, Curtis pressed me against him, covered my mouth with his, stifled my voice. Surprise, affront, disbelief and something else, gave him immediate mastery. The kiss was expert and prolonged. On his side, totally emotionless. Cold in its way as the dead diver's mouth. I could feel his unaccelerated heartbeat against my breast, see the calculating glitter of his wide-open eyes.

Background noises mixed with the angry riot of my own heart. A brief ribald cheer from the group of men behind us, a remark in slow Cornish dialect about that being the sure certain way to treat a woman. Then everyone in true British style ignored us. Conversation resumed about the lobster-fishing, the rough old tides they'd been having, and the first big match of the football season. There was the clink of glasses, the rattle of bottle tops, the ringing of the cash register. Fill her up, same again, a woman's voice querulously demanding another Guinness. Vasha's gay girl laughter. Still the kiss went on.

I could see in close-up the tanned skin stretched tight over his high cheekbones, the thick dark hair haloed against the jazzy light, his curly black lashes. The living kiss resurrected the dead one, awoke memories and feelings I'd been unaware of possessing.

I stopped wriggling and lashed out viciously with my foot. I heard it make contact with Curtis's shin. As his grip momentarily slackened, I lifted my hand and smacked his face hard.

Afterwards I wondered why I did that. I could have got away from him then without it. That slap was an expensive luxury, a self-indulgence, a sop to my pride. A reply to his humiliation of me. Not just because he'd kissed me, but because he'd kissed me like that.

I saw his head jerk back. His hand go up automatically towards his cheek. But he remained calm. Untouched. A curious unreadable expression glittered in his narrowed eyes. His only reaction as I climbed off the stool, he leaned forward and whispered, just loud enough for me alone to hear, 'Get to hell out of this.'

The last I saw of him, he was examining the red handprint on his cheek in the tinted mirror and grinning exaggeratedly rueful. He turned and said something to the group nearest us. And the same Cornish accent drawled, this time on my side, 'You had it coming to you, Jack, that you did.'

Their comfortable beery laughter followed me to the door. I didn't see Vasha. The swing door shut behind me, cutting off their voices.

I stood outside in the cool sea-blown air. The pavement was shiny with a fine mizzling rain. I held up my face, feeling the soft needles cool on my flushed cheeks. I pressed my lips together. Tasted that kiss again. I began to run blindly head down, into the rain. Knowing I had to escape. But not knowing then from what.

I hurried down the cobbled cul-de-sac, across the High Street, and on to the promenade. I lowered my head to keep the drizzle off my face. I could hear the furious clacking of my high heels ringing in my ears – but from far away as though those feet were someone else's. Nothing to do with the real Olivia, the clear-headed sensible girl, now dispassionately trying to analyse Curtis and all his words and works.

Sitting there, his cheek scarlet from a girl's smack, trying to pretend it was some lover's quarrel, would he think I had fled to implement his advice straight away? That in half an hour's time I would be back on the road to London? Leaving whatever was going on down here into which I had unwittingly slipped to work itself out to its conclusion?

Who did he think I was? What sort of person? Why was my absence so desirable?

One thing was certain, the missing device, Scorpio as William called it, was somehow at the bottom of everyone's strange behaviour. And Curtis was implicated in it right up to his neck. He wanted me out of it. And he was perfectly prepared to lie, fake, plead, deceive and probably a good many other things to get rid of me.

Why?

I turned left up the road to the parking meter where I'd left the car. The rain was heavier now. Great grey clouds were coming in with the tide, their hems mingling with the spindrift off the wave-crests. Water coursed down the gutters, gurgled through the grilles – a sad sucking noise in tune and mood with my own thoughts. What did Curtis know about me? Quite a lot of facts since he had listened to the police questioning. And he had been interrogating me ever since.

What did *I* know of Curtis? Next to nothing. He owned a new black MG of this year's registration, with a fine expensive radio and headset. He had no permanent home in this country, though he had mentioned something about a flat. He had worked abroad for a number of years but he hadn't pinned himself down as to country. He had said he was looking at a sailing school with a view to purchase. Profession – this and that.

Family? None that he had mentioned. Footloose and fancy free. The sort of man who travelled light. He had lots of friends and acquaintances, though. People to greet him in pub or police station.

He had spoken to someone as soon as he heard my story, and then pretended that the telephone was out of order. He had spun some sort of yarn to the stupid police sergeant. But what *after* that? Who actually removed the body? Why did they dump it where they did? What happened between then and the time that Curtis found it? And had it shaved and presented to me as evidence that it ***wasn't*** the one I had found? Why was it so important to him that I should accept his version? Why when deception failed did he try to silence me then and there? Scare me away?

'This your car, miss?'

A policeman again, faceless under the helmet, rain dripping off his cape.

I nodded.

A jerk of the head towards the meter, now indicating orange penalty, a scatter of raindrops. 'An hour and twenty minutes after expiry . . .'

A notebook first, then a blue pencil. Trickling smudges on the paper. Answers from me, explanations. More questions – on and on, while the rain dripped down steadily over the two of us. I remember thinking to myself even then, is he doing this deliberately? I felt that no matter what I did in St Edzell's I was bound to get in badly with the police. It was like being the dunce of the class. The butt for teacher's jokes. For some reason the police had it in for me. Why should a policeman do all this anyway? Why not one of the innumerable traffic wardens? And then, finally, just when every question of illegal parking had been asked, suddenly out of the blue, 'You been drinking, miss?'

He leaned down close to me. The face had a little brown moustache drowning now under the wet pink nose. The policeman's expression turned from severe to very nasty. In the museum there is a sixteenth-century wheel from Sicily, the thick rim beautifully carved and painted with the faces of the villagers from where it came – peasants, landowners, soldiers, priests, girls, matrons, farmers – all smiling and pleasant and honest. But when the wheel turns, a most strange change of expression – the smiles fade, craftiness, deceit, cruelty come up with the movement, blurring with the speed, the faster the wheel turns the greater the transformation. Only at the hub is a man's face, quiet, peaceful, wise, never changing. I have thought, in the secret recesses of my mind, that some day I would recognize such qualities in some man's face. And that . . .

But ever since I came down to St Edzell's, it was as though I saw faces – Curtis's, the sergeant's, Mrs Luxford's, Vasha's, William's, now the policeman's, at first with the wheel not turning, and then, as events propelled it faster and faster, faces changed, their expression altered, their words had double and treble entendres, the kind intentions became threats and forebodings. Was there anyone at the hub who would never change? Certainly not the police. There was a time when they were Mr Plods, kind directors of the way to the lost, wonderful to foreigners. Now they were suspicious, disbelieving, stupid, and increasingly corrupt. Probably a few of them were mixed up in something too. It wouldn't be the first time. Whose side were they on? Certainly not mine.

'Oh, but you *are* in charge of the car. You have the keys . . . I wouldn't take that attitude if I were you, miss.'

In the end, after warnings about summonses and things that could be coming to me, he let me go. By that time, in spite of the rain, I was hot and furious. I managed to contain myself sufficiently to drive slowly through St Edzell's, I wanted no more charges slapped against me. And I didn't tread hard on the accelerator until the last bit of the coast road to Mrs Luxford's.

I jumped out of the car and then nearly tripped over a shiny red bicycle parked against the railings on the other side of the gate. I hurried up the path, opened my handbag, groped for the key.

I felt my compact, my lipstick, my perfume phial, a few stray coins – no key. I rummaged around again, pulled open my bag, peered into it. The key wasn't there. I felt in the pockets of my coat. Nothing. I stood on the doorstep trying to remember where I'd put the key. I hadn't taken my bag down to the beach yesterday, but up in my room I'd transferred the key to my slacks' pocket. That's where it was – in the wardrobe up in my room.

It was a good thing that Mrs Luxford was home. I walked round to the rear and found the back door slightly ajar, the door from the kitchen to the living-room shut.

There was a tea-tray on the kitchen table, set for two with the best china, scones and home-made seed cake. A fragrant smell of cheroots leaked through from the living-room, despite the closed door. Mrs Luxford was standing on a stool with her back to me, reaching a tin of biscuits down from the top of the cupboard. As I came in she turned her head quickly and nearly fell backwards.

'Sorry. Did I give you a fright?'

Sighing, she climbed down heavily from the stool, pressed her hand to her left bosom. 'I didn't expect you so soon,' she said, glancing at the closed door. 'And you don't as a usual come in this old way.'

'I couldn't find my key.'

Pink already, Mrs Luxford's face went red with suppressed annoyance. She muttered about not liking keys being lost, not with so many burglaries and nasty happenings that you read about these days.

I had the impression she'd have spoken more sharply if it hadn't been for the visitor behind the closed door.

'It's not lost, I left it in my pocket upstairs.'

Slightly mollified, she arranged chocolate biscuits on a plate, and said with an indulgent smile, 'You're as bad as

Vasha. Always losing her key or leaving it in the wrong coat. Too many clothes you young girls have now. Don't never learn how to look after things. Like my little mothers at the clinic. Mr Wragg and I were just saying . . .'

'Mr Wragg?'

A coy smile. A deepening flush, an almost skittish toss of her head. 'My caller.' She poured the boiling water into the pot. 'Take the tea things in, m'dear, and come and meet him.'

I picked up the tray.

'He's just popped round to say he's been appointed circuit steward. Isn't that nice?' She opened the door and propelled me through.

The air in the sitting-room was dense with the same fragrant tobacco smell. Sitting in the fat armchair with his back to the window a slight ginger-haired man was puffing away at his cheroot as if putting out a smoke screen. He rose as I came in and advanced towards me. He walked with a sidling stoop as if a south-west wind blew him – a narrow-shouldered, foxy little figure with pale eyes and a ragged red moustache. He took the tray from me and set it on the table.

'Miss Browning, a pleasure.' He clasped my hand, 'I'm Archie Wragg.' The reedy moustache parted to show long teeth. The voice purred like Red Riding Hood's wolf himself. I'd guess he was in his late fifties, not a very healthy-looking chap with bloodshot eyes and a purply veined skin. The lean and hungry type, now rubbing his hands together unashamedly at the sight of that laden tray.

Frayed cuffs to his shirt, shabby suit, not given to spending on clothes. Besides cigars, he smelled strongly of whisky.

'Well, now you two've met, sit yourselves down, the pair of you!'

Mrs Luxford waved me to the armchair opposite the window, and pulled up a hard-backed chair for herself between us. She stirred the pot, and passed the plates and asked Mr Wragg about next Sunday's hymns, and if they'd got enough helpers for the Harvest Festival garlanding. Then she asked archly and unnecessarily, 'Shall I be mother?'

'I can think of no one better, dear lady.' And while he sugared his tea, he remarked on the mysterious ways of the Almighty who passed over such as Mrs Luxford and called to the sacrament of motherhood such itty-bitty-chitties as the naval wives.

'Not fit to be mothers, the half of them!' he said to me. 'Met any, have you?'

I shook my head. Not just in answer to his question, but because I'd got that odd feeling of double entendre again, of being in some way manipulated. I felt that Mr Wragg's presence here, and even the apparently casual conversation, were part of someone's purpose.

'Mr Wragg works up at Pendragon. He knows them all.'

The feeling deepened.

Yet the next moment, I was just as sure I was wrong. 'He's the welfare officer up there.'

'For my sins.'

'Mr Wragg, I really don't think you have any, that I don't!' She beamed on him with such unfeigned approval that I began to wonder if Vasha's was, in fact, the only romance going on beneath this roof. 'He's a real saint,' she whispered behind her hand.

'Have you any family yourself, Mr Wragg?' I asked.

He was dredging tea through his moustache. He stopped, shook his head and put down his cup. 'I'm still waiting for Mrs Right.' There was another fond exchange. 'Mrs Right for Mr Wragg. Good, eh?'

'Very.'

'But he understands the young as if he had a score of his own.' Mrs Luxford refilled his cup. 'Ever so kind and good he is to our little mothers. Keeps a real fatherly eye on them.'

'Grandfatherly more like, dear lady. Itty-bitty-chitties of seventeen and eighteen. They need a smack on the hand. But I listen to them.' He stroked a red ear. 'I let them talk it out of their system.'

'All they ever do, seems to me,' Mrs Luxford sighed.

'How were they today, dear lady?'

'Upset, some of them were. Only natural. Jenny Baines, the wife of one of the HSL crews, is due Friday. Says she's hardly seen sight nor sound of *him*.'

'It's always the women who suffer in time of war.' Mr Wragg's intonation was that of a lay preacher. Then he shut his lips tight as if he'd said more than he intended. His blue eyes rested on my face, inviting my comment.

I said nothing.

'I refer of course to the Cold War,' he said as if I'd asked him a question.

I nodded.

'Like the poor, it is always with us.'

I nodded again.

'Time was when the war frontier was the Berlin Wall.'

'But not now?'

'No.'

'Where, then?'

He gave a deliberately baffling foxy smile, and a shrug. He turned his foxy pointed profile so that his eyes rested on the greying sea.

'Out there?'

'Could be.'

'Is it true, Mr Wragg, about the Russian trawlers?'

'I don't say yes and I don't say no. I tell a lie. I do say, yes. There are Russian trawlers. Just as there are French and German and Belgian and Dutch. And maybe Italian and Greek, and Albanian and Panamanian too.' He buttered a scone and pointed his knife at me. 'And maybe some of them are not being good Jameses and Johns, the sons of Zebedee. *Not* following the calling of true fishermen. But getting up to hanky-panky.'

He popped the scone in his mouth. I sipped my tea and watched him over the rim of my cup. He helped himself to another scone and ate greedily. He seemed to have forgotten what he had begun to say.

'Poor Jenny Baines.'

'Who, miss?'

'The girl who's due.'

'Oh, her. Not to worry. She'll get her better half back in time. They'll have found it by then.' A crafty look at me. Another deliberate mistake.

'Found what?'

Mr Wragg smiled broadly. 'Oh, come, come! If you're telling me you don't know, you must be just about the only person in St Edzell's who doesn't.'

'You remember, Livvy. Course you do! What William said. They've lost one, from Pendragon. Scorpio misfired.'

'It didn't misfire.' Mr Wragg leaned forward. 'I tell you no secret and I tell you no lie. But in confidence, miss. Because you have an honest face.' He dabbed his mouth with a handkerchief. 'At the critical point of the drop, in came one of those . . . well, wolves in sheep's clothing . . . and interfered.' He paused. 'So off it's gone now like one of this dear lady's new-born babies without its mum.'

The simile visibly moved Mr Wragg. The watery blue eyes glazed.

'Can't it cry out?'

'Muted. No signals coming from it. Lying somewhere helpless for any Russky or Chink to come and sweep up.'

'And that's what you're looking for?'

'Oh, not I, miss! Those strapping lads that fill this dear lady's clinic for her.'

'Why is it so important to find it?'

Mr Wragg let out a quick bark of laughter. 'Let's just say it's of urgent national importance, eh? Secret . . . and we must keep our secrets secret. Security slogan, miss . . . one of our better ones. And what the little chap homes on is secret too.'

'William's already told us,' Mrs Luxford said. 'Something to do with sound.'

'It's a bit more subtle than that, dear lady. But William's a bad lad. He talks too much.'

'What about you, Mr Wragg?' I asked softly.

'A good question. But that's different. What bit I've told you is just to help you. Get the record straight. Isn't that what they say? Besides, it might just assist you remember something you forgot.'

'About what?'

'When you walked last Thursday evening.'

'I've already told the police everything, and they didn't believe me.'

That same Sicilian wheel began to turn again. Mr Wragg's smile tightened, the corners of the foxy mouth drooped. 'Of course they can't believe you, miss. They know that body couldn't exist.'

Faster.

'They can check with the Admiralty and find out if there were any divers around there at the time. They know. So it's up to you to keep quiet. Stop saying things like that. Otherwise you never know, you might just get a little smack on your little hand.'

'Well, we all let our imagination run away with us some time, Mr Wragg,' Mrs Luxford said mildly.

The wheel stopped. The smile came back. Surely I had been mistaken.

'That we do, dear lady. Specially when we're artistic like this beautiful young lady here. I hear you work in a museum in London. Not thinking of going back from this Garden of Eden just because of a little misunderstanding, miss?'

I said I would be staying for my full fortnight's holiday.

'Good! Excellent! No doubt you have other interests here. Do I not detect your eye anxiously on the clock?'

'Going out, are you this evening, Livvy?'

I nodded.

'Then you best be getting changed.'

Mr Wragg stood up. 'Ah, to be young again!'

He made a few more flattering remarks to the pair of us, and then Mrs Luxford showed him out.

'Well,' she said, 'and what did you think of him, then, Livvy?'

I wasn't sure, so I said, 'Very nice.'

She seemed disappointed. 'Speak up, Livvy. Say what you mean.'

I hesitated, then I quoted a bit of Cornish I still remembered, '*Byth dorn re ver dhe'n tavas re hyr*,' the rough translation of which is *too long a tongue, too short a hand.*

For a moment she said nothing. Then she said, 'You're wrong, Livvy. He's got a long reach, has Mr Wragg. Let us hope, m'dear, that you don't find that out.'

I lay a long time in my bath. It's the Freudian place to think.

And I badly needed to sift together in my mind the kaleidoscopic fragments of the day and make at least some semblance of pattern.

Mr Wragg had been surprisingly informative. Suspiciously so, I might have thought. But I dismissed that suspicion from my mind as a symptom of the strain of the last few days. I now felt more certain of myself. To feel more Olivia than Ophelia. I was beginning to exchange my illusion for their collusion. Though I didn't know who *they* were. Nor whose side *they* were on. And if the natural concomitant of this was that I would certainly then be in danger, it didn't strike me with the impact that it ought to have done. Given the choice between suffering hallucinations or being in danger, most people would opt for the latter. No illusion about one thing anyway – my key *was* in my slacks.

I was towelling myself dry when the front door bell rang. I heard Bryan's voice and then Mrs Luxford calling upstairs that my friend had arrived. Voices continued as I went through to my room to dress. I heard Bryan's easy unforced laugh, Mrs Luxford's buttery accent. Vasha's name. Then mine.

I took my dark blue dress out of the wardrobe and laid it on the bed. I opened the dressing-table drawer for my fresh underwear. I paused with my fingers poised over the neat piles. I am a neat person. I knew exactly what order those piles were in this morning. But now that order was slightly changed. A pair of black pants was on top of the pile, the blue ones halfway down. Someone had been through my things, maybe searched the whole room.

I sat for several seconds at the dressing-table. Below me, I heard Mrs Luxford and Bryan come through into the kitchen. I heard her demonstrating her electric mincer. I heard the back door open. My window was wide. Their voices floated up. Bryan was assuring Mrs Luxford that yes, it really had stopped raining, and no, he wouldn't mind getting his shoes wet, and yes, he would like to see her chrysanthemums.

Their two heads appeared below my window. They walked down the path. He was wearing a tweed suit and a brown shirt. He looked reassuring, solid, kind.

I called down that I wouldn't be long. He turned, looked up. 'So that's where you are, Olivia!'

He smiled with unfeigned pleasure. The thought of the room being searched lost its impact. At least *he* was the same.

It is fifteen minutes' drive into St Edzell's, and I talked all the way. I hardly noticed Bryan's silence, except that I knew it was sympathetic. I told him the whole story, from the beginning. I told him about my walk on the beach, finding the diver, the lift from Curtis, stopping at the box, the telephone call, the police's scepticism, what the sergeant said, my search for evidence, the piece in the newspaper, the attempt to pass off the body as someone different, the policeman by the parking meter, their ganging up on me, and now my room searched, and the over-friendly behaviour of Mr Wragg.

Bryan heard me out before making any comment. His only reaction as I spoke was his foot pressing harder on the accelerator, giving physical expression to his anger and concern. The Lotus's powerful headlights leapt ahead of us. Trees and hedges blossomed, died behind us into the darkness. Our tyres hissed over the damp road.

When I finally finished we were coming through the outskirts of St Edzell's. He slowed, and asked, 'Is that everything?' A pause. '*Now?*'

'I think so. I may have left bits out. But that's more or less it.'

Bryan lifted his foot right off the accelerator. Ran a hand through his hair. 'What I don't understand is why you didn't tell me all this yesterday?' His tone was reproachful, almost offended.

'I don't know. I suppose I was afraid.'

'Of me? Olivia! Really!'

'No, I wasn't afraid of you. I was afraid you wouldn't believe me.'

The car slowed to a crawl. The supermarket and the sub-Post Office went past our windows in slow motion. He took his left hand off the wheel and touched mine.

'I know what you mean. I understand, really. But I'd always believe you, Livvy. I have a very special reason for believing anything you happen to say. I did just think that you might feel the same about me. But that's by the point. And now isn't the time to tell you.'

I said nothing. I had some idea what he meant, but I didn't press him to elucidate.

'Special reason apart,' I said after a moment. 'Do you still believe me?'

'Implicitly.'

'Thank you.'

'I'd only have to look into your eyes. The sergeant's a fool.'

'Oh, he is.'

'And this what's-his-name, Curtis, is a downright rogue.'

'Yes.'

'And someone is greasing someone's palm.'

'Not mine.'

'Nor mine, alas.' He sighed. 'Look. I was going to take you to the White Horse now. But after today, would you rather not?'

'I'd like to go.'

'I must say I'd like another look at the famous or infamous Vasha.'

'Oh, she's not infamous,' I exclaimed. 'Far from it! I like her. *And* I trust her.'

'No, you don't. You *know* you don't. You don't really trust anyone but *me*.'

I shook my head. But I didn't speak. We had reached the top of Beacon Hill. St Edzell's spread out below us – the melon slice of the bay, the half-pendant of promenade lights, the coloured blobs of the butterflies and the bunches of electric flowers. Their combined incandescence cast a sheen on the swollen sea so that it looked like the dark three-quarters of the moon to the little bright crescent of the town.

'Pretty,' Bryan said. 'So harmless-looking.'

'But it isn't.'

'No.'

We drove slowly down the hill, past a queue waiting outside a fish and chip shop, past a souvenir arcade and the Bingo Hall. Another queue there. Some sailors and their wives. You'd have thought they'd had enough excitement for the day.

As we reached the beginnings of the promenade, Bryan said, 'Hence your willingness to risk life and limb to get that handkerchief?'

'Yes.'

'I'd wondered about that. I thought it must have been someone very special who gave you that.' A brief smiling glance. Undertones to his voice.

'Well, now you know.'

'Yes, now I know.'

'I thought you were the scientific unromantic type?'

'So I was.' A pause. 'Got it with you, have you? The hankie?'

'Heavens. I wouldn't carry that around. I threw it away.'

'But I thought it was important?'

I felt the slenderest thread of disbelief in me now running through his measured kindly voice.

'Not in itself. It couldn't tell me anything. Just that it was there. I'd used it then. So I must have been there.'

He laughed. 'I see. True female logic!'

We went slowly along the promenade. The traffic lights were against us. We halted. He covered my hand. Together we watched a black sea break white in the lamplight, send a thunder of tall spray cascading over the railings. High tide. About this time two days ago, an unknown man had been thrown up by that same sea. And who he was, where he had come from, how he had died, what he was doing, if in fact he existed at all, remained a mystery.

The sea is very like that painted cartwheel. It changes face with every turning of the tide.

'So you're satisfied there *was* a body? Oh, yes. I know what you're going to say. My boys had seen divers. True.'

'And we know there's a missing device. So he was looking for it.'

'What if he'd found it?'

'He couldn't have. If we'd found it, the search would be off. If anyone else had found it, they'd have scarpered. William said that.'

'William? Oh, yes. The driver chappie.'

'We might see him too tonight. He's always hanging around Vasha.'

'Or the other way round?'

The traffic lights had turned green without our noticing. A driver behind us blared his horn. We swung left and left again into the White Horse yard. It was already half full of cars. While we went slowly up the cobbled cul-de-sac searching for a place big enough for the Lotus, I glanced round to make sure there was no sign of Curtis's car. Even with Bryan with me, I was nervous – my female antennae doing their best to warn me again.

Bryan parked the car neatly, and switched off the engine. But he didn't move. In a fastidious schoolmasterly manner, he said, 'Now let us go over what we know.' He counted off our pieces of information on the fingers of his left hand. 'A sonar device is missing. The drop was interfered with. The device is secret, and valuable. Important that, Olivia, because people act differently when there's a lot at stake.'

'You're thinking of the police sergeant, aren't you?'

'I'm thinking of no one in particular. I'm stating a fact.' He paused. 'To go on. At the same time, you find the body of a diver. Nationality unknown. Could be anyone. Your evidence is supported by divers seen by my boys.'

'Thank you. *And* my hankie.'

'Exactly. But denied by the police sergeant who may first have been contacted by Curtis. A proven liar.'

'Correct.'

'The search on the beach is deliberately delayed. The body vanishes. You are advised to forget about it.'

'Curtis again.'

'The disappearing body then reappears miles away. And while you're out, delayed by Curtis and/or the police, your room is searched, and you have this odd confidential conversation with, of all things, the Pendragon welfare officer, Mr What-was-his-name?'

'Wragg.'

Bryan stopped talking and clasped his hands. Slowly he said, 'I think the body was removed in order to confuse the issue. The possible location of the device.'

'How was it removed?'

'Well, there was heavy rain before you and the police returned to the beach. That could have obliterated footprints.'

'Which side removed it?'

'Maybe the ones who interfered in the first place.' He smiled faintly. 'When in doubt, use mathematics.'

'How?'

'Find the common denominator.'

I didn't have to think long.

'Curtis,' I said. 'He's the common denominator.'

'He is indeed.'

'From the beginning . . .' I said. But Bryan wasn't listening.

'It's just possible that certain people think you, Livvy, are the common denominator.'

'Such as who?'

'I don't know. Curtis again, perhaps.'

'He wants rid of me.'

'I wonder *why*? If he thought you knew something, wouldn't he want to keep close to you?'

Bryan opened the car door and came round and opened mine. I got out and stood on the glistening cobblestones. I smelled the salty tang, felt the prickling on my skin of sea mist. Tiny droplets of moisture frosted the street lamps. The beginnings of the fog.

'He told you to go back to London?'

'Yes.'

Bryan locked the car thoughtfully, put the keys in his

inside pocket. He took my arm as we walked up to the White Horse.

'Tell me, does Curtis know your address in London?'

'I don't know. Oh, yes, he would! He heard me give it to the sergeant. If he remembered, that is.'

'He'd remember. Does he know you live alone?'

'Yes. I suppose he might remember that too.'

'Then for God's sake don't do as he suggests.' Bryan stopped me and put his hands on my shoulders. His voice was urgent though he tried to smile. 'It's just possible he might want you, well, *more permanently* out of the way.'

In the light of what followed that night his words had an almost prophetic ring.

'Promise me,' he said, 'that you won't trust anyone but me?'

I promised him. It wasn't difficult. And then we went inside.

The saloon bar was half full and brightly lit. The bar no longer an empty stage, but all part of it. Customers leaned on the bar counter. There was the clink of glasses, men's voices. Vasha's laughter. A small fire burned in the imitation inglenook. Cigarette smoke hung under the lights. I could just see the ash-blonde top of Vasha's head as she pulled beer, reached down glasses, flattered the women, teased the men.

I thought I heard a voice that sounded like William's, but I could not see him in the crowd. Bryan and I found some empty stools at the far end of the bar.

'This do you?'

I nodded.

Bryan took my coat, hung it up, asked me what I'd like to drink. Something told me I was going to need a cool head tonight. I asked for cider. Not from the wood, but bottled.

Vasha took her time about coming over. She was busy, of course. But she made time to have a good look at Bryan in the mirror first.

She must have liked what she saw. She was all smiles, when she came.

'You've been in before.' She extended her pretty little hand. 'I would not forget a face as handsome as that.'

'I came in once,' Bryan said, quite overwhelmed by her. 'I'd heard they had a very attractive girl in here.'

She made some remark about Bryan having a smooth tongue too, and though it wasn't true, it didn't seem to displease him. She also made a crack about me and meeting up with seductive men.

She didn't mention Curtis, nor did I. She took our orders, shook her head to Bryan's offer of a drink, said she had them stacked in front of her down there. Much as she'd like to, she couldn't stay with us long. William was being . . . how you say it? . . . possessive.

'I thought I heard his voice,' I said.

'Sometimes I think I have heard nothing else. And his accent is not pretty. Birmingham. You do not come from Birmingham, Bryan?'

Bryan laughed and shook his head. 'William's your boy-friend, is he?'

'To speak the truth, Bryan, I do not know what he is to me. Tonight I think he is one big silly nuisance.'

'Tell him to come and have a drink with us,' Bryan said, doing the decent thing as usual. Though I knew he didn't want William any more than I did.

'May I really? I would like that. You are very kind.'

She stood on tiptoe and beckoned. William must have been sitting at one of the little tables by the bar watching her in the mirror. I saw his brown head and big broad shoulders jerk up above the rest of the crowd. He pushed his way forward obediently with those loose puppet movements. He stood beside Bryan, arms dangling, face fixed into the semblance of a smile. Waiting, I thought, for the next jerk of the string.

' 'lo, Ollie.'

Bryan winced.

'Mr Wayne, I would like you to meet my affianced friend, Weelyum Hardaker. We hope one day to be married. Weelyum, this gentleman is a friend of Livvy's, Bryan Wayne.'

'We had a noggin t'other evening, didn't we, sir? You're the beak bloke.'

'So we did. Take a pew, William. Have a drink.' Bryan assumed a jolly schoolmasterly tone. 'And congratulations.'

'On what, sir?'

'On your wedding plans. Your engagement.'

Weelyum shrugged, but said nothing.

'Now what's it to be? I'm in the chair.'

William sat down, put his elbows on the bar and asked for a scotch, double if sir's kitty ran to it. Bryan ordered it for him without batting an eyelid.

'Weelyum works up at Pendragon.' Vasha set the drinks in front of us.

'That must be frightfully interesting, William.'

'Frightful, maybe. *And* something else.'

'What?' Bryan winked at me.

'Dangerous.' William had obviously started his drinking when the bar opened. 'Very dangerous.'

Vasha stifled a giggle a bit too late.

'Bloody dangerous!' William gripped Bryan's arm. '*They* –' he looked from Vasha to me – 'those coupla birdies . . . don't understand.' He lowered his voice. 'We're working on anti-sub neuk stuff.'

'Really!'

'Stuff that the Russians would give Stalin's sacred tooth for.'

Vasha laughed out loud. 'Buddha! Buddha's sacred tooth!'

'Who the hell cares whose tooth? They'd give it.'

'I'm sure they would, William. But it's up to chaps like you to see they don't.'

'How can I stop them, if the big brass let 'em muck up the drop?' He stared gloomily into his whisky. 'Could be anywhere.'

'Big thing to lose.' Bryan winked at me again.

'No, it's not. I know. I tell you for why. I've seen Scorpio. I tell you, that little monster's no bigger'n a nice size codling.'

Another giggle from Vasha.

'Well, cheers, Vasha, Olivia, William!' Bryan said with tactful haste. 'Happy days!' He raised his glass. 'I'm sure it will turn up, William. If enough chaps are looking for it.' He might have been talking to the Upper Third about a lost cricket ball.

His soothing tone had the opposite effect on William.

'There are too many bloody sods looking for it! What d'you reckon those trawlers are doing out there? You must've seen 'em, sir?'

'Well, I've seen trawlers, William.'

'But those are special ones. I tell you. Pendragon tracks 'em! Has to. Oh, you girls can laugh! But this place is full of people on the look-out.'

'You might well be right, William.

'Too true, I'm right!'

'But don't you have very tight security?'

'Oh, sure, sir. Like they had at Harwell. Like they had at bloody Portland. Like they had all decent chaps and kiss my musical, up at the Foreign Office with Mr Vassall. Not to mention the real high-ups, Burgess, Maclean and Philby. So what do we have here to keep us all safe? A boozy little lay preacher, who's the welfare officer besides. *That's* security for you!'

I managed to stifle my own exclamation of dismay at Mr Wragg's role in this. And yet some part of me heard that piece of information without surprise. Here was another face that was not quite as it seemed. The wheel had turned again. The friendly welfare officer had become the suspicious security officer. And yet he had *deliberately* given me information.

Why?

I had no time to ponder. I saw a purply-pink shiny hand descend on William's shoulder. I heard a thin voice say, 'And who taketh the name of security in vain?'

Mr Wragg was with us in person.

By mischance or careful design, there were still some empty stools this end. Wragg didn't ask if he could join us. He simply sat down. And under the excuse of fair do's, inserted himself on the other side of me. He offered us all a drink. He seemed unabashed by Weelyum's remarks. His only emotion, delight that we had seated ourselves in front of a bowl of those white shiny cocktail onions, which he immediately began to crunch.

'Actually,' Bryan said as he proffered them to us, 'Olivia and I are going to have supper.' He had now the look of a man who has had as many uninvited friends as he can take.

'There is lobster salad tonight, Livvy,' Vasha said. 'It is

very excellent. Local caught. All very fresh and succulent.'

'By a happy coincidence, I am eating here too. My landlady – ' Mr Wragg turned to me – 'is an excellent woman – a pillar of rectitude. But a lamentable cook.'

'Do you not go home to your wife, Meester Wragg? At the weekends?'

'Alas, my dear, there is no Mrs Wragg. Never has been. I have remained a bachelor my whole life through.'

'Like Weelyum!'

Mr Wragg raised his eyebrows, drew a deep sighing breath, but said nothing.

There was one of those speaking silences. Mr Wragg selected an onion, popped it in his mouth and sucked it. Weelyum squirmed on his stool. Bryan attempted conversation. He asked Mr Wragg if he liked St Edzell's.

'Frankly, no, brother.'

'Have you been here long?'

'Too long, brother. And you?'

'I'm just holidaying here.' Bryan told him about the boys. That endeared him to the old fox. He expounded on the good clean life. Plenty of games. Boys' Brigade and all that. Had had a corps once himself. *Mens sana.* Bit of army discipline never hurt anyone.

'Well, my boys don't get exactly that.'

William said treacherously, 'I'll say they don't. Wander all over the shop.'

'You must bring them to chapel, brother. They'd get a rousing welcome. Nothing I like better to see than rows of well-scrubbed lads.' He picked an onion skin out of his teeth. 'Nor hear better neither. Plenty of good singing. We've some real strong hymns for tomorrow . . . the Old Hundredth.' He hummed: ' "All people that on earth do dwell . . ." marvellous. What's your favourite hymn, miss? How about "Abide with Me"? That always gets 'em going . . .'

I was saved from making a choice by Vasha's return. She was carrying a tray with four platters of lobster salad. Mr Wragg helped her eagerly. She set a cloth on the counter, knives and forks and silver lobster picks, and a pitcher of salad dressing which she said she had mixed herself. She seemed to take it for granted that William would have supper with us. My over-active antennae sensed that in some way we were being manipulated. But if so, surely only very harmlessly. And if it was to help Vasha, did I really mind?

Mr Wragg and William concentrated on their food. Bryan gave me an apologetic little smile and a shrug. We made an odd foursome, I thought, looking at our reflections in the bar mirror, all eating in silence, dipping our heads over the plates, crunching the radishes and the crisp lettuce, picking out the pink lobster claws. The Sicilian wheel spun. I looked again. The shiny ranks of bottles looked like cage bars. We were four silly hens, pecking away at the last feed before the chopper descended.

Then just as the empty plates were all cleared away, and William was jingling the coins in his pocket as if he was going to buy us all the coffee, the saloon bar was opened with a flourish, and Curtis came in.

It was five to ten. I looked at my watch because I saw him look at his. He saw me too. Our eyes met in the mirror and the look should have splintered it. If the reflection of a face can shake with anger, his did. Only for a second. The wheel turned. The angry face smiled, though not in my direction.

Curtis walked to the centre of the bar. He asked in a loud voice, 'Time for a quick one?'

'It's almost on closing,' Vasha smiled. 'But of course for a friend!'

I engineered another reflected peep at his face. He looked pale, his nostrils pinched.

He paid for his beer, lifted his glass to his lips, looked around over the rim of it, the way lonely drinkers do, as if for casual company. He saw us, and raised his free hand.

Immediately Mr Wragg beckoned him over. But Curtis was coming anyway. On the other side of the bar, Vasha accompanied him. The customers that end all had full glasses. The lady in the purple hat sat solitarily at a table contemplating her Guinness. A couple of men shouted goodnight, stood for a moment in the doorway, pulling up their coat collars. A wisp of fog and sea smell drifted in as they left, vanished in the smoke and the heat of the room.

'Come and join us, brother.' Mr Wragg intoned it like a hymn. 'You look cold.'

'It's damned cold outside now. Fog.'

'Thick?'

'In places.'

'Then warm yourself on good fellowship, brother. Vasha, don't forget that coffee. Make it five.' Mr Wragg began on introductions.

'Livvy I already know,' Curtis said, eyes on me. And without pause. 'I thought you were going home?'

'Going home, brother? Dear me no! She's only just come! Isn't that right, miss? Now you don't know Mr Bryan Wayne. He's here on holiday. What did you say your calling was, brother?'

'Schoolmaster.'

'Excellent, excellent! An honourable calling. No wonder you know how to discipline those young tearaways.'

Mr Wragg put his shiny hand on Weelyum's shoulder.

'I know Hardaker,' Curtis said, and nodded brusquely. He then went on to say something quite unforgivable. I think at one time I might, if there had been some good reason for them, have forgiven him his lies, and his deceit. But this, never. He seemed to me to pause for a moment, to wait till Vasha was returning with the coffee tray, and well within earshot. Then he asked in a loud hearty voice, like an actor declaiming his lines, 'How's your wife, Hardaker? Is it true she's coming down here tomorrow?'

Vasha stopped in her tracks. Her mouth gaped, her eyes widened, her hands shook. Who was the slack-stringed puppet now? The cups, the coffee-pot shivered on the tray. The scalding liquid spurted over her hand. For a moment she seemed too confused to know what to do first. It was Bryan who reached over and took the tray from her. Mr Wragg who mopped up the spilled coffee. Vasha stood for a moment, her eyes filling with tears, her mouth still soundlessly gaping. Then she pressed her scalded hand to her lips, and still without saying a word, lifted the bar counter flap and fled to the Ladies' Room.

Both William and I followed her. He grabbed her free arm, as she reached the door, spun her roughly round, imprisoned her with both his big hands flat on the door panels either side of her.

'Listen,' he said, 'you know bloody well . . .' His face was mottled red. He'd had too much to drink to be able to cope with the situation. He was incoherent. 'If you . . . I'll . . .'

He leaned right down and whispered something.

It was I who pulled his arm aside to release her, my voice that asked coldly, 'You'll what, William?'

But only Vasha's ears heard the last few words he said, though *I* saw her face.

I closed the door of the Ladies' Room behind me, and stood with my back to it. There was a frilly-skirted Formica-topped dressing-table opposite me, with a pink vanitory unit beside it. Vasha subsided on to the matching stool, her hand still pressed to her mouth.

'It's best to hold it under water,' I said. My own voice sounded cool, insufficiently sympathetic perhaps. Vasha looked up at me quickly, tossed her hair back from her face. Her mascara had run, her eye shadow was smudged.

'Your hand,' I reminded her.

'Oh, *that*.'

'Is it blistering?' I walked over and touched her shoulder.

'My *hand* is not blistering.' She indicated a deeper seated pain.

I turned on the tap of the washbasin. 'Cold water takes the sting out. Unless you'd like me to go to the kitchen. They're bound to have burn dressings there.'

She wouldn't hear of it. 'No, please, Livvy . . . stay! It helps to talk to a friend.'

'Put it under, then.'

She swivelled round on the stool, and held her hand under the tap. She left it there as if she had lost all interest in it. She tilted her face up to me, tear-stained, anguished. She was an easel showing a portrait of grief. As soon as I thought it, I was ashamed.

'It is not about my hand that I weep.'

'Because of William?'

A nod.

'But did you really want to marry him? I know it's difficult for anyone else to judge . . .'

'It is impossible,' she interrupted me, 'for anyone else to judge.'

'But he doesn't seem . . .'

'My type?'

'Yes.'

'Don't you know that women sometimes fall very passionately in love with exactly the wrong type?'

'Yes,' I said. 'I do. Indeed I do.'

Something in my tone made her look at me intently. Behind the blind of tears her eyes were sharp.

'All the same, I don't think you're in love with him.'

'You being such an expert,' she said, and then, 'I'm sorry.' Looking back on it, I can see now that she changed her tactics slightly then. But that's hindsight. One can never sort things out clearly in the emotion of the moment. 'I promise you, Livvy, I wished very much to marry him. I was *counting* on marrying him.'

'Damn Curtis!' I said.

'It is not his fault. I had my suspicions. Before now.'

'You're better off without William really, Vasha.' I expanded on the age-old theme of men being deceivers ever. Of there being more fish in the sea than ever came out. Finishing up with, 'You're so attractive, Vasha, you'll soon meet someone else.'

At that point she shook her head and real genuine tears flowed. She looked less and less like a painting of grief, more and more like someone very naked. Someone seen without disguise. Someone in need of unspecified help.

'But there is not time.' Her eyes flicked past me to the door.

'For what?'

'You do not understand.'

'Then help me to.'

She hesitated. 'In confidence?'

'Of course.'

'Swear?'

'I swear.'

She took a deep breath. 'I am in trouble.'

'Through William?'

She nodded.

'Are you pregnant, Vasha?'

She hesitated again, and then shook her head. 'But how can I explain, because of what I find out, tomorrow I must do two things. And I cannot at the same time do both.'

'Go on.'

'So I need help. I have so few friends. I used to think I could ask Weelyum to do anything.'

'But I'm your friend, Vasha.'

'Yes, that is true.'

'So ask me.'

'Anything?'

'Anything.'

'Promise?'

'I promise.'

It all seemed so simple. So much less of a tragedy than Vasha had at first led me to believe. In confirmation of my assessment, Vasha's sobs shuddered away into nothing, as if her emotions had been held too long in the wrong gear.

'I'm glad there's something I can do,' I prompted in the ensuing silence.

'It's an errand. Not a large errand.' She smiled. 'It is a pleasant drive.' The smile faded. 'But you must do it exactly as I tell you.'

'Of course.'

'And tell no one.'

I shook my head. Then a disquieting thought struck me, the prim English maid. 'Is it legal?'

'Oh, quite legal.' A faint contemptuous smile. Where the swinging decadent British?

For my part, I already regretted my offer. More than my offer. My promise. 'What is it then, Vasha?'

She kept her eyes on the door behind me, and said, 'Listen carefully.'

I did as she told me with growing impatience. I even began to hope someone would interrupt us. The errand was somehow so like Vasha itself. 'Couldn't you post this envelope?'

She shook her head. 'I do not yet know who must have it.'

I shrugged.

'You will take it? Yes?'

'All right.'

'You do not now regret your promise?'

'No, no. Of course not,' I said with the vehemence of untruth.

I saw her look sharply at the door. The handle was turning. The middle-aged Guinness drinker in the purple velvet hat came in. She nodded good evening, waddled slowly over to the lavatory. The bolt shot. Cravenly I wished she had picked a time five minutes earlier to come in.

The party had broken up. Wragg and Curtis had gone without waiting to say goodnight. A sullen, guilty William penitently collected glasses. Bryan stood by the bar, my coat over his arm, relaxed and patient. He was jingling his car keys. He had his eyes on the door, watching the trails of fog come in with every departing customer. There were only a few left. A group in the far corner, draining their glasses. A middle-aged man I hadn't seen before warming his hands by the remnants of the fire. The purple-hatted lady came out of the Powder Room behind us, and joined him. They went off arm in arm together.

'Sorry to keep you waiting,' I said to Bryan.

'That's all right.' He smiled, called, 'How's the hand, Vasha?' as she hurried by us, head down.

'Better.'

'Beastly things, scalds!'

He asked her if she'd like a lift home with us, though he didn't press her when she refused, and I didn't blame him.

I put on my coat. We said our goodbyes. Outside was a wall of fog. It bent back the bar-room lights behind us, hushed the traffic sounds. Bryan took my arm.

'Cold?'

'Not particularly.'

'You're very quiet.'

'I didn't mean to be.'

'Sorry about this evening.'

'Why should you be?'

'I'd intended it to be a twosome.'

He was gently piloting me between foggy shapes parked along the cul-de-sac. The pavement was slippery. Water tinkled loudly down a drain. Somewhere a foghorn sounded.

'Requiem for an evening,' Bryan said.

'But I enjoyed it.'

He stopped me under a street lamp, and grinned. 'What with uninvited guests and a broken engagement thrown in?'

'An engagement that never was,' I said, and shook my head. 'Didn't *you* enjoy the evening?'

'Oh, of course I did. But then I was with you.'

I didn't know how to answer that.

'And you're Vasha's friend. You've obviously taken it to heart.'

'Not really.'

He tilted my chin and stared by what light there was into my face. The lamp shone out in yellow fuzzy beams like the spokes of a velvet-ribboned wheel. Vasha had worn a different face tonight. Once again, the wheel had gently turned.

'I must say – ' he held my arm tighter as we walked on – 'I didn't envy you in there with her.'

'Nor you outside with William.'

'Oh, he was all right. Just pole-axed.' His voice smiled. A car nosed its way past us. Yellow fog lamps bathed us briefly in painful brilliance. 'To my nasty schoolmasterly mind, there was rather more to that than met the eye.'

'Slavonic temperament,' I said. 'That's all.' Prim English maids kept their prim English promises. Even from their best friends. Vasha would have been proud of me.

'Never mind Slavonic temperament, how's that for British navigation?' Bryan's hand slapped the nearside wing of the Lotus.

'Spot on.'

He eased himself round the bonnet and unlocked the doors. Then he switched on, letting the engine run a bit to warm her up. The windscreen wipers snapped back and forth like twin metronomes. Counting the seconds before something.

'They seem a pretty ill-assorted pair,' Bryan laughed.

'But who can tell what's a well-assorted one?'

A pause. 'You and me.'

Then feeling perhaps that he had said too much, he began to ease the Lotus away from the kerb.

Fog smoked in the turning headlamps. The thick tyres hissed along the cobbled street and then out into the crawling traffic of the High Street. The junction lights were red again. It felt a long time since we had stopped here before.

'It seemed to surprise you that Archie Wragg was a security chap?' Bryan said suddenly, resting his hands on the wheel.

'A bit, yes.'

'Any special reason?'

'It's not what he said before. He told me he was the welfare officer. Maybe the two go together?'

'Maybe.'

'Perhaps the more you know about the staff's business, the better?'

Bryan laughed and said the ways of bureaucracy never ceased to baffle him. Tailor-made for Blakes and Pontecorvos and Houghtons and Philbys and Fuchses.

'Wragg isn't any of those.'

'But how can you be sure?'

'I can't really. But he *is* the security officer.'

'Listen, Olivia. What do all those names I just reeled off haphazardly have in common? And God knows there are others too.' The last was drowned in the upsurge of the engine as Bryan accelerated when the green light shone. We turned right on to the promenade in a squeal of fast tyres.

'I don't know.'

'They were all on the *inside*. Employed by the British Government.'

'Oh, Lord!'

'And well you might say it.' As always when he was worried, his foot pressed hard on the accelerator. Empty parking bollards flicked past us. *All on the inside*. I thought of the sergeant and the policeman who'd deliberately delayed me today. I thought of Wragg. I thought for a long time of Curtis. I asked myself again . . . what besides a liar was he?

'So how can you be sure of anything and anyone?'

'How indeed!' I thought of the dead diver and Vasha and Mrs Luxford. All changing. All different. And I thought of the sea invisible behind the railings. Ebbing fast now. Not even a drop of spume coming up to show its presence. But there.

'How can one be sure of oneself?' But I didn't say it

aloud. Weren't there other faces on my wheel? What of Olivia, Livvy, Ophelia – which one was me?

Above our heads the summer illuminations garish as Pendragon's unnatural lights stained the mist with their flower and butterfly colours, before they too vanished behind. Ahead of us, suddenly a muzzy red light. Then another. A car going fast in the same direction. We hung on to its tail for a while.

We overtook it, halfway up Beacon Hill, and went roaring away. The fog thinned patchily at the top. Our headlights picked out the wet fronts of dark buildings, glistening pavement. Then as suddenly mist clapped over our eyes again.

'You think you see a bit. Then, back at square one again,' Bryan said, changing into second gear. But he wasn't just talking about the fog.

'It'll lift eventually.' I wound down my window. House lights floated disembodied. I heard the foghorn again. A snatch of music from someone's television. We met a couple of cars along here, St Edzell's bound, following their own twin crinolines of light, nosing forward cautiously.

'So Curtis wants you to go back to London. And Wragg doesn't?' Bryan said suddenly. 'Interesting.' We were coming up to the new part of the highway and the big yellow light standards.

'What d'you make of it?'

'A severe conflict of interest. Could they be on different sides of the fence?' He smiled, accelerated. The huge lamps cut through the mist like a detergent through grease. We sped along.

'What *I* have to do is make sure you're safe. If only we knew as much as some of our drinking friends knew.'

'You think they're all in it?'

'In some capacity or other. I should think a quarter of the

population here are indirectly concerned with Scorpio.'

'But all above board.'

'Ninety-nine point nine per cent.'

The lamps fell behind us. Fog again. Autumn trees dissolving in the mist. The brightly lit vanishing square of the fateful telephone-box. We crawled along again. Bryan was silent and thoughtful. I was touched by his concern for me.

He saw the turning before I did and swung off the road. We dipped into a white surging sea of mist. If the two were synonymous in his mind, it was right that the fog should be thickest here. He nosed forward cautiously. Mist smoked in the dipped headlamps, swept over the bonnet. Nothing else showed. The tyres spat and churned on the sandy surface. Grit spattered the body with tiny, disproportionately loud taps. Then on my left, a hawthorn branch fronded in mist.

'All right this side,' I said.

'I can just see the hedge here too.'

'Will you be all right getting back?'

'Of course. Don't worry about *me*.'

Ahead I saw a delicate brisé fan of light sticks from the cottage. Someone must have heard the car. The fan closed a little as a light snapped off upstairs.

We crawled up to the gate. The curtains downstairs were undrawn, but no Mrs Luxford came out to meet us.

'Will you come in for a coffee?'

'I'd love to. But maybe better not. This stuff's liable to get worse. Besides, you should go to bed. Have an aspirin and a hot drink. I'll come and see you tomorrow if I may. Forget about everything till then.'

I promised I would. He waited in the car till I walked up to the front door. Mrs Luxford had left it on the latch, so she must be still awake. I waved goodbye to Bryan. I stood in the doorway to watch him turn. I waited till his rear lights dissolved in the mist. As I let down the catch, I heard the distant roar as he accelerated out of the lane.

I shut the door behind me. Mrs Luxford had left two flasks on the kitchen table. I unscrewed mine. Hot milk. I drank it gratefully. I left the light on in the kitchen for Vasha and went upstairs. Light rimmed Mrs Luxford's door. Her voice called out to me. She asked if I'd enjoyed myself and if I'd remembered to slip down the catch.

I closed my bedroom door. I felt uneasy. The room was cold. Fog had crept in through the open window. It hung under the light like some ghostly reminder of problems unsolved. I pulled down the window sash, and for once, bolted it. I drew the curtains tightly shut. I undressed and crept in between the icy sheets.

I was tired. But I only dozed. I kept waking with a start, listening for something.

It must have been hours before I heard what I waited for. The sound of a heavy vehicle coming up the sandy road. The clicking of the gate. Then the key in the front door, Vasha's light hurrying footfall on the stairs. Her room door closing behind her.

Then I fell into a deep sleep.

Sunday

I woke to a knife of bright sunlight through the curtains, the cry of gulls. Downstairs plates rattled. I smelled bacon and toast. Jumping out of bed, I pulled back the curtains and opened the window.

I saw high stacks of dazzling white cloud in a blue sky, the landscape clean and sharply etched, the moor purple, the new cement of Pendragon sunlit as a Spanish resort. Salty sea air stirred at the curtains. A smart wind was getting up. It blew in the intermittent ringing of church bells. No foghorns this morning. No ships' bells. Not even a helicopter. The colours of today were clear and harmless. It was like cleaning off the siccative and varnish from some dark gloomy oil painting, and finding beneath the fluidity and brilliance of a Turner landscape.

I looked at my watch. Close on ten. I picked up my sponge-bag and went to claim the bathroom before Vasha.

I had no competition. Not a sound from her as I dressed and went downstairs. Mrs Luxford was washing up with her best hat on, the pearl pin ready to be fixed, a beady eye on the clock.

'What time is the service?' I asked her after our good mornings.

'Eleven. Shall you come, m'dear?'

'I thought I'd stay and have a chat with Vasha. But I'll run you down.'

She shook her head. There were friends who picked her up at the bottom of the lane at ten-thirty. She'd set off presently. Our breakfast was in the warming oven. She and I would be having cold lunch, but if I liked to set the table before she got back from chapel, it would be kind.

'Vasha's egg'll be set as stone,' she said, fixing the veil with the big pearl pin. 'There, even yours looks a bit on the hardy-side.'

'D'you want me to give her a shout?'

'Would you, m'dear. I've given her a knock once. She's on at the White Horse. But you know what she's like.'

I ran halfway up the stairs and called.

No answer.

'Leave Vasha to me,' I said, handing Mrs Luxford her gloves. 'Off you go. I'll see she has breakfast and gets to work.'

She checked in her purse to see she had her collection money, and went briskly down the lane. The sound of her footsteps died. The house settled down in silence.

Vasha had been late in and she probably needed her sleep. I ate my solitary breakfast. I looked around for a Sunday paper. But none had come. I washed up. By this time, Vasha's bacon and egg were worse than hardy. I threw them into the waste-bin. I got out another egg and another rasher from the fridge. But before I cooked them I took the precaution of calling out again, 'Vasha. Breakfast.'

No answer.

This time I walked upstairs and tapped on her door. 'Vasha, you'll be late. I've promised I'll get you up. Now come on!'

I banged on the door. It rattled on its hinges.

'Vasha! Get up.'

I banged louder.

'Vasha.'

My fingers closed over the handle. Then I hesitated. I

remembered last time I had gone into Vasha's room. I didn't want to see William there again.

'Vasha. I'll come in and get you up.'

I put my ear against the door. Surely she couldn't be that dead asleep. Surely she'd have answered now? Surely I'd have heard something, a creak, a rustling, a protest?

I hammered with both my fists on the door. I nearly broke the panels. Explanations gabbled through my brain. She'd come in late, she'd maybe had too much to drink, she'd been depressed last night and she just didn't want to surface. Or perhaps she'd got up already and gone out.

Simple explanations flooded in, but my heart had begun to hammer as loud as my fists.

I turned the handle and walked straight into her room.

Vasha was there all right. There was a large hump in the bed hidden by the green eiderdown.

Gently I shook it. As though it was alive under my touch, the eiderdown began slithering on to the floor, revealing Vasha's feet, her slim ankles, the black frills of her nightdress, her arms by the side of her body.

And then in glutinous slow motion, I saw a lumpy knot of plastic underneath where her chin should have been. But no chin, no face. Her head, her pale hair, her cheeks, her eyes all still blurred as though in last night's fog, caught inside a steamed-up plastic bag.

I tore at it, pulling it aside, seeing bright purple cheeks, open, staring, sightless eyes.

I took her hands. They were ice cold.

A sort of numbness came over me. I didn't cry or call out. I stood there trying to get my mind to work out what to do.

Then slowly I went downstairs. As soon as I opened the outside door, the sun dazzled my eyes.

There was nobody around. Only the seagulls, wheeling in the blue air above me.

Looking way down the hill, I saw a man with a brown bag on his back, pushing a bicycle.

I started to run. My feet slithered in the sandy lane. I called out to him. I was panting so much I couldn't get any words out.

The newspaperman's face was red and sweating. He thought I was complaining about the paper being late. He said something about it not being worth his while to deliver, not really, only did it as a favour to Mrs Luxford. He unhitched his bag off his shoulder, began to delve inside.

'It's this old hill that takes it out of you.' He brought out a *Sunday Express* and handed it to me.

I just shook my head. I couldn't say anything. I couldn't explain. I could only pull him away from his bicycle, into the house, up the stairs, through the door of Vasha's bedroom . . .

He was a nice man – fatherly, kind, sensible. He made me go into the living-room and sit down. He rummaged in Mrs Luxford's sideboard cupboard, and produced a glass of neat brandy.

I was the sort of girl men plied with liquor, I remember thinking, but not for the usual reasons. For a few minutes his unhurried footsteps echoed quietly round the house. Then I heard him pick up the receiver in Mrs Luxford's room, and start dialling.

The police again – and more questioning. The same sergeant, the same policewoman. Familiar figures in a nightmare now. They eyed me sceptically. Smiled without warmth, as if I were some strange bird, some dead albatross bringing death and disaster. A police surgeon was added to the cast, in a black overcoat and with a midwife's black bag. He hurried past me, eyes lowered, as I sat in front of the empty grate opposite Mrs Luxford. Someone had snatched her out of chapel and driven her home. She still wore her hat, held her gloves nervously, smoothed out the fingers, said nothing.

For hours we sat like that. All the time there were comings and goings, soft-voiced questions. A kind of belaboured police sympathy for Mrs Luxford, as she stared ahead out of the window, eyes filling up with tears, fixed on the sea. I felt frozen, as if the icy touch of Vasha's hand had somehow entered my bloodstream. I kept rubbing my fingers together to get the circulation going. Till once, almost accusatively, Mrs Luxford asked, 'Why d'you do that, Livvy?'

Momentarily the policewoman stopped scribbling and looked up, and I flushed guiltily.

The questions were resumed. They wouldn't take long, the sergeant said. Routine, really. The ballpoint made a dull squeaky sound on the paper. Mrs Luxford mustn't distress herself. Kindness itself to give the girl a home just like that.

'And how did you come across her in the first place, Mrs . . . ?'

'I put an advert. In the *Western Morning Mail* – Doctor Penfold said I should have company. And the money's been handy.'

'What sort of tenant was she? Did she pay her rent regular? Keep her room nice?'

I listened and didn't listen. It was like being back at school, and hearing another pupil's oral exam before yours. Knowing you wouldn't get the same questions. Hoping you'll do as well.

On went the questions. Did she have any men-friends? Was she engaged? Where had she been before this? London was a big place. Whereabouts? Did Mrs Luxford know if she was, well, what they called these days, permissive?

'Not in my house, *no! Never!* Not anywhere else for that matter to my thinking.'

Did Mrs Luxford know of any quarrel, worries, troubles, family matters that might prey on the deceased's mind? Had she any family? Did she get letters? Did she write to anyone?

Then it was my turn. A bit less sympathetic. Too many bodies or supposed bodies around me in too few days. Already I had a reputation.

'Were you alone in the house when you found the body, miss?'

'I was.'

'You were also one of the last to see the deceased alive?'

'One of the last, yes.'

'How was she then? Was she cheerful?'

'Not very.' I gave them a brief account of the incident in the bar. Until then the errand that Vasha had given me to do had been pushed to the back of my mind. The memory of it brought me up sharp. I hesitated. Decided to say nothing.

'She was hoping for marriage then, was she, miss?'

'So it would seem.'

'She didn't mention her work permit?'

'No.'

'Or her return to Czechoslovakia?'

'No.'

'And when you came in last night, you locked the door behind you?'

'I dropped the catch, yes.'

'The deceased had a key?'

'Yes.'

'And you heard her come in?'

'Yes.'

'So the house was all locked up after she got back?'

'I presume so.'

'And what time would that be?'

I said I didn't know. He asked me if it was possible I might have dreamed it. In all fairness, I said I supposed I might though I didn't think so.

Mrs Luxford chimed in that I'd had some nasty dreams since *that other night*. Then the questions stopped.

In the silence that followed there was a lot of tramping on the stairs. The heavy awkward steps of men carrying something. They were taking Vasha away. I gripped my hands together. Mrs Luxford closed her eyes. The tears squeezed from the corners of her lowered lids, and ran an uncertain, hesitating path down her wrinkled cheeks. The front door opened. Sea air blew damply in. Footsteps diminished down the path. Lowered voices instructed one another. Car doors slammed. Engines started, swelled, and died away.

A guilty feeling of relief overwhelmed me.

Someone made tea, the policewoman I think it was, or Mrs Luxford's chapel friend. Sandwiches too, though nobody ate anything. I drank the warm sweet liquid greedily. I began to feel life circulating again in me. I looked at the clock on the mantelpiece. It was almost ten to two.

The sergeant stood up. Like a little ink shadow, the policewoman stood up too.

'Well,' he said, addressing himself to Mrs Luxford, 'it's all been a very distressing old business. Leave everything, will you, as it was, in the room? Don't shut the drawers nor nothing. There'll be some lads coming up this afternoon.'

The two of them walked across the living-room.

'Would you like me to send up the doc to give you a little something?'

'What for?'

'To make you sleep.'

She shook her head. Then he looked at me, I shook mine.

'Right then.' He nodded to us. The policewoman said 'Goodbye,' with an uncertain smile.

The front door opened and shut again. The last police car moved away. Mrs Luxford stood up and began to unpin her hat.

I walked slowly upstairs, past Vasha's closed door, into the bathroom. It was there, just as she had said it would be. Tucked into the crack, where the old medicine cupboard, loose on its screws, was not quite flush with the wall. A thick white envelope, slightly squashy and padded, holding more than just a letter.

Gently, I eased it out of its hiding-place, and slipped it into my pocket.

The direct route from St Edzell's to Minack is via St Buryan and Gweal – but I took the roundabout devious way on the unmade roads over the moor.

I am not naturally devious, but the events of the last few days had made me so. I'd told Mrs Luxford that I must get away for a while on my own. The atmosphere of death and dismay in the house gave my excuse credence. She said she understood. Her friend from chapel was going to stay with her. Presently they would sing a few hymns. I was young. It was right I should get out. Fresh air would do me good. But I must promise I wouldn't be long, since now she feared 'for you, Livvy'.

It was late afternoon when I left. All the time I was driving I kept looking in the mirror, watching for cars following. I was certain a police car tailed me to begin with, but I shook it off in the one-way streets round the market-place. Then I thought a white Cortina attached itself, but I doubled back, and it disappeared on the Land's End road. Perhaps it was all imagination – but this time particularly it was important that no one knew what I was doing.

In the empty seat beside me was last Friday's *Western Morning Mail*, taken from the shelf of Mrs Luxford's broom cupboard. Still in my pocket was the sealed envelope. Vasha had been explicit. On no account was the envelope to be opened. It was to be folded in that edition of that newspaper and deposited in the wire refuse basket by the third row, centre aisle, of the auditorium in Minack Open Air Theatre. It must be dropped there at five-thirty and I must leave straight away.

I turned right past Wheal Fortune. The empty sockets of its windows and the gaunt doorway gaped at me. Ivy grew round the chimney of its engine-house, thick stemmed and luxuriant leafed. It was in flower. The knobby greeny-white blossoms garlanded the slender dangerous structure like a maypole.

Since I had remembered the errand today, I had been trying to rationalize what I should do. When you are asked to help someone in obvious distress, you can't refuse. Last night there hadn't been time to ask questions. Was someone blackmailing her? Putting the pressure on her? But why had she sent me on the errand? Why *me*? Why was it important to her? Was it me for want of someone better? Me, because she knew she wouldn't be able to do it herself? Me, because she had already resolved on suicide? If so, what purpose did the errand serve?

Not revenge, surely. In these days of letter bombs and miniaturized explosive devices, the thought froze my blood. I must have eased my foot off the accelerator for the Triumph slowed. My face broke out in a cold sweat. A mud-spattered mini pick-up van appeared over the crest of the hill behind, came up close. I kept going slowly, watching him in my mirror. He overtook. There was a piece of farm machinery in the back. I let him get out of sight before I accelerated again. There was a long straight stretch of narrow road. I went fairly fast because time was getting on.

The clouds were gathering up, daylight shrinking. Slanting sun gleamed on stubble fields and autumn-tinged hedgerows. The sky was empty of aircraft. A flock of whimbrels circled. Soon they'd be migrating. A sign of winter coming.

I took the left-hand fork up the farm road past the Caradoc salt pits. If this errand were not personal, not revenge, what then? That Vasha was not what she appeared now seemed obvious. She was caught up in something – as others clearly were. Beneath the placid surface of blessed St Edzell's, under the make-up of popcorn and bathing and trips round the bay, of church chimes and bazaars and boy scouts, of roundabouts and Big Dippers and swings, was something ruthless and sinister. A struggle, a war perhaps as bitter and savage as the sea itself.

I had studied the envelope, felt its padded squashiness, held it against the lamp in my bedroom. The glow coming through the paper revealed no writing. Should I open the envelope and look inside? My fingers had hesitated. But Vasha had specifically asked me not to, and Vasha was dead. I was burdened with a now even more solemn obligation than the one I had unwillingly assumed last night. And whose correct carrying out was my responsibility.

On my right now, a dip down into a disused china-clay quarry. I turned the car, drove it up into the shelter of gorse and bracken. I made sure it was out of sight. Then I locked it. The landscape was empty. I began to walk the three-quarters of a mile over the heather to Minack.

Tell the police – that had been my strongest inclination. But then I had thought again – the stupid sergeant, the pretty policewoman, the rest of them. Their disbelief of me, their seeming belief of Curtis. For all I knew, these fears that kept revolving inside my head were just imaginings. The envelope might contain nothing more than some private token to be picked up later by William in the romantic surroundings of Minack. I remember her telling me she'd been there with him in the summer. I shuddered to think now, after her death, of police fingers on something like that. Maybe it was a bundle of his letters returned? Or maybe the fact of his marriage was not as surprising as everyone thought. Maybe she had intended to carry on the affair. Maybe she had *not* decided on suicide till later.

For suicide it was. The sergeant had said as much. Foul play was not really suspected. Couldn't be ruled out, of course. But as good as. The method gruesome and grotesque, yes – but if he might say so, typically female. Painless, relatively. More certain than drugs, for these days they could bring you back marvellously with ten times the lethal dose. Quick as hanging.

Straight ahead now the path between the heather marched south. The moor was deserted. Some bird, a plover I think, squawked up from a hollow of bracken. I saw a red tractor moving, slowed by distance beyond a small stone cottage on my right. The ground rose gently, the path climbed. Suddenly in front of me, the glitter of the sea. An inshore wind was coming in quite hard against my face. The sun, low in the west, coated the high granite cliffs with gold. And now I came to the end of the moor, and on to a twisting road from which sprang a narrow lane to the cliffs. *Unsuitable for heavy traffic.* There was a white painted wooden signpost *To the Minack Theatre.*

The lane was narrow and corded with old wheel tracks. Before I walked down, I looked around for anywhere that a car might be parked. There was a cottage right on the roadside, tightly fenced, and further away, a field of winter wheat with a padlocked gate. There was always the moor, where if you knew it well enough a car could be hidden like mine in the gorse and the bracken or beneath a stone sheep shelter. Always supposing that whoever came would come by car.

I looked at my watch. Five o'clock. I intended then to carry out Vasha's order to the letter.

The lane was muddy, the tracks filled with water from Cornwall's wet summer. The tarnished pools mirrored the dark dappling of the evening sky. There were the recent marks of sheep and a dog's paws, but the human footprints were old and blurred. I walked on the side of the lane where there was coarse grass, not altogether to keep my feet dry.

On the left now, a granite house all shut up against the Atlantic gales. I stood and looked at it carefully. The gravelled drive was empty. There were no tyre tracks. The lock of the iron gate was stuck with rust as if it hadn't been touched for months. I stared up at the windows. The only movement there was the reflection of the slow march of cloud across the Atlantic sky.

I turned away not completely satisfied. Did someone live there? Could someone even now be watching me? I walked slowly across an empty car park towards an empty wooden ticket office. A box no bigger than a pigeon coop. A couple of gulls squabbled and screamed on the ledge outside the little shuttered window. I suddenly felt terribly vulnerable and terribly alone.

On the loose stone walls behind the booking office, torn

posters flapped in the smart breeze. I straightened one, held it up against the wall. It announced the last play of the season, *The Tempest*, by William Shakespeare, to end definitely on September 10th.

I had never been to Minack before. I had imagined the usual open-air theatre, grass and bushes and stones and a pretty lake – The Rose Bruford or Regent's Park or at school where we had listened, uncomprehending and bored, to plays in Greek, sitting on mackintoshes on the damp hard ground.

This theatre simultaneously enchanted and terrified me. A few steps from where the grass and heather ended, it was as if the whole cliff had given way, not violently, but gracefully and artlessly to form a natural amphitheatre. There were rows and rows of stone seats in a semi-circle, intersected by stone steps and stone aisles in the traditional curve of a Greek theatre, leading to a smooth rock for a stage that looked as if it had been there for fifty million years. The wings were piles of boulders, their massive planes gilded and shadowed now in the sunset.

But most dramatic of all was the backcloth. The great drop of mingling sea and sky, with the wind whipping up the crests of the green-grey Atlantic rollers. Across the water, the battlements of high Cornish coastline, shadowed by crevasses and caves and sentried by a rocky island pockmarked by seabirds. I walked on, and peered down. A sick-making drop. The waves in shadow here were greeny-black, rushing in white-plumed to crash against the rock, the noise echoing like gunfire against the granite walls.

There was nobody around. No one in the lane, no one on the heath but the distant tractor-driver. No ship on the sea. No aeroplanes, no helicopters. No sheep, no dogs. Nothing but gulls and gannets between me and every horizon –

north, south, east and west. Only an awesome loneliness – a solemn cathedral-like atmosphere in which the music was the cry of the cormorants, the beating of my heart, and the thundering organ chords of the Atlantic below.

I could imagine *The Tempest* being performed here as in no other theatre in the world. The storm, the shipwreck, the drownings – all were here. No need of scenery, no need of costume. No need perhaps of actors or words. Just the sea.

Half forgotten fragments of *The Tempest* came into my mind – 'What have we here, a man or a fish, dead or alive?' 'legg'ed like a man and his fins like arms . . . this is no fish but an islander that has lately suffered by a thunderbolt.'

I thought of the dead diver and shivered.

Here on these curved seats thousands had sat enthralled. On that rocky stage, hundreds had declaimed, acted, mimed.

Now there was nobody but me. And soon, somebody else.

Who?

And acting what, in what sort of drama?

I stepped down the rocky slabs of the aisle carefully. Now the place reminded me of something else – half of that Sicilian wheel. There on the top was the rim, and now I was walking down the centre spoke to the hub. I could see the wire basket by the third row, exactly as Vasha had described it.

The steps were deep. I walked slowly. I glanced repeatedly behind, half expecting to see a figure outlined against the horizon. For suddenly I realized that here at Minack my wheel had stopped, petrified in stone. Here I was sure I would see one of those faces and that it would be the true face, undisguised by changes, happenings, dissembled loyalties. I began to think, too, that if only I could see the real face I would understand why Vasha had died. Maybe even unravel my own mystery. Till that moment I had not really questioned what I would do. Now it seemed clear and obvious. In my heart, I thought it must be William. In a way I hoped it would be.

It would explain so much. It would make things less sinister. Sad and pitiful, yes. But separated from the happenings at Pendragon and the weapon.

I walked across the proscenium and up on to the stage. The wind whipped my skirt against the back of my legs. It sighed in the funnel of the rocks beyond the wings. I walked a few paces and such are the acoustics that the scrape of my shoes rustled among the stone seats of the auditorium like opened programmes.

I stood in the middle of the stage. From left to right, I slid my eyes on all those empty rows.

No one. Nothing.

On the left and right there were rough areas beyond the stone rock columns of the wings, which were clearly used for dressing-rooms and lights. I explored the theatre all over. Down the south-easterly side is a steep winding path, dotted with sea pink and small gorse. I went right down to where it ended in a ledge five feet or so above the water. I stood there on the wet granite ledge, as wave after wave came up and exploded in white shrapnel over my shoes, and the spume blew wet in my face.

I knew now that I had to wait here. I knew I had at least to try to find out who would come. I trusted no one enough now blindly to carry out orders. I put my hand in my pocket and felt the letter's soft yielding substance. Layers? Of gun cotton? An explosive device? A letter bomb to be detonated on opening? Even if it were a remote possibility I couldn't just leave it there to kill. I explored the wings on the westerly side. One large rock on top of two others, a kind of scooped-out cave. Then a steep drop. A shiny granite weathered cliff beyond a grey stone slab stained with greasepaint. The last sunrays were full in my face, the waves a glittering emerald green. Over the rich mineral sea bed the spray splintered into rainbows. Then the cloud banks closed. The sea darkened. The spume came up, driven in by the wind, a cold pool of purple shadow settled in the proscenium.

I looked at my watch. Five-thirty.

I shivered, partly with cold, partly with excitement, partly with apprehension. I stepped down from the stage. Acting was over. I crossed the proscenium, walked to the centre aisle, stepped up, and lifted the lid of the refuse basket.

It squeaked. It smelled of oranges. There was some crumpled pieces of skin curled and leathery, there for weeks, a cigar packet, cigarette ends. I folded the newspaper, then folded it across again, as Vasha had told me. I dropped the paper inside the basket and shut down the lid. I had the curious feeling, nerves no more, that someone was watching me. That someone waited for me now to continue up the steps, past the booking office and the car park, up the lane, and away.

Instead, I fled like a shadow to the right-hand wings. I had already decided where I would station myself. I crouched on the stone slab, hidden from the amphitheatre. I had an excellent view of the whole stage, the centre aisle, the basket, and the entrance to the theatre. Anyone coming in would be skylined full in my vision. I would see them cross the car park, and walk by the ticket office, a minute at least before they reached the basket. Thinking time. Time to decide how to act.

I watched and listened. I strained my eyes in the gathering twilight. The wind constantly deceived me. A dried leaf rustling over the stage sounded like a step on the granite chippings of the car park. It whistled sharp as a signal in the organ pipe of rock. A big wave broke deep and vibrant as the horn of a vehicle.

I looked at my watch again. Six-fifteen.

I began to wonder what I would do if nobody came. How long would I wait? What about Mrs Luxford? Why was I so certain that I would find out something?

But now I was beginning to wonder just how much I would be able to see if anyone did come. There would be no moon for hours yet. The amphitheatre was a halved cup of shadow. The little hut of the booking office a black cardboard cut out against a greeny-violet sky.

Behind me, the island gleamed a dull white in the darkness with settling sea birds. They crooned and squealed and flustered. A handful of sea spray came up over the slab with the rising tide.

Seven o'clock.

I wriggled myself more comfortably. I scraped at the greasepaint with my fingernails. I wondered who had used it, what part they had played, what they looked like. I missed the first faint sound, or I disregarded it.

Then I heard it again. And again. The crunch of feet on gravel. Feet walking quickly and firmly, not bothering to disguise themselves.

I shuffled nearer to the crack between the rocks. I pressed my eye to it. Did the actors thus wait for the right cue? What cue did I await? I held my breath, listening. I tried to gauge from that meagre thud who it might be. I knelt right down and put my ear to the rock floor, Red-Indian-like. Sound vibrates through rock.

A man's tread. Slow, unhurried. A man's tread pausing somewhere out of sight. An agonizing pause. My heartbeat lurched in a queer rocking-horse rhythm. I pressed my hand to my mouth in an agony of indecision. What if he simply went away? Should I come out and look?

Then the steps started up again. A dark silhouette appeared on the horizon. A man in what looked like a belted raincoat. Hatless. Tall. My heartbeat quickened.

Could be a policeman. Could be William.

Then, unmistakably, something in the way he turned. Head up, unhurried, arrogant.

Curtis.

I watched him come down the centre aisle. His face was a pale glimmer in the darkness, glancing to the left and right. Without hesitation, he stopped at the basket. I saw the gloves on his hands as he reached down very carefully for the newspaper, extracted it, held it in his hands. Then infinitely slowly, he began to open it up. Methodically, unbending first the horizontal fold, then the vertical, then opening it to the centre page.

Finding nothing.

Again he put his hand down into the wire basket. There was the flicker of torch. It darted like a phosphorescent bat into the basket, on to the lid, the area immediately round the basket, then along the seats, across the proscenium, on to the stage, the wings. Torch and face came my way. I shut my eyes, moved my face from the crack, curled myself flat as a lizard to the stone.

Now I daren't look. I just cringed and listened. I heard his steps echo on the stage. I heard him walk up and down, caught the quick reflected flick of the fearful torch. Then the torch went out. I heard the scrape of a match, smelled it. Caught a drift of pipe smoke. Thought wildly, maybe close as this, he could smell my perfume?

He stood there for minutes. Then he whistled a snatch of

some tune. Vaguely familiar. I tried to think where I'd heard it before. Of course, at the White Horse, that lunch-time . . . *no more money in the bank.* Was it a signal? Or just a gesture of defeat?

Then he turned. I heard his heel scrape. He must have passed right beside my crevice in the rock. He leaned on the stone slab and stared down at the sea. I caught a glimpse of his profile in the glow of his pipe. I could have stretched out a hand and touched his raincoat.

Then abruptly he knocked out his pipe. I saw the little red-hot embers dance off the rock. He dropped his pipe in his pocket. Turned again, passed out of my vision.

I listened, head down. Footsteps getting fainter across the proscenium, continuing up. Fainter and fainter, a repeat of before, gravel, sand, turf.

Then, marvellously, very far away, the sound of a car starting up. Accelerating. Moving away. Fading into nothing.

Again I was alone in Minack. All the same I waited for another half-hour before moving. And when I did, I moved like a guilty shadow. I glided out from the cave in the rock. I was less surefooted than when I came. I trembled with delayed shock and the surprise of reprieve. I kept to the darkest parts of the theatre, moving up the side aisle, crouched low to the ground.

The wind had moderated, but the sky was overcast. I kept to the side of the lane again, hugging the wall, freezing at every darker shadow.

I found the path, a dark straight parting in the glimmering turf and heather of the moor. I found the disused quarry, the cones of clay ghostly white. I found my car, screened by the gorse-bushes. There was a light powdering of whitish dust on one side where the wind had blown up the loose clay particles.

With relief I got in, and started up. I didn't try this time to take the devious route, but drove straight home. I kept my foot relentlessly down on the accelerator. I can't remember anything of that drive, except darkness, blossoming headlights, and a kind of numb dismay.

Even so, it was ten past nine when I got back. Mrs Luxford had the front door open as soon as she heard the car.

'Where have you been, m'dear?' She drew me inside. Her friend from the chapel switched off the television, the better to listen to me. I could think of nowhere I might have been on a Sunday evening. I said I had driven on and on, and then lost my bearings. True, in a way.

'We've been ever so worried, Livvy.' Mrs Luxford stared at my sodden shoes, my muddied skirt, my ripped tights. 'And that nice Mr Bryan Wayne . . . twice he's been on the phone . . . worried sick he was, said if you weren't home soon he was going to call the police.'

I was touched by Bryan's concern, but I was thankful he hadn't gone to the police. The police wanted no more of my escapades. And now I wanted even less to do with the police.

They had been proceeding all afternoon and evening with their enquiries and investigations, Mrs Luxford said. Very thorough they had been, and very satisfied were they with their results. An open and shut case. The Inquest had been called for tomorrow afternoon. Surprisingly quickly, yes. But delay wasn't necessary, and only caused distress to relatives.

'I thought she hadn't got any.'

'She has. So it would seem. An aunt some place. I can't pronounce it. In Czechoslovakia anyway. That's one of the reasons they want to get things cleared up quick.'

I said nothing to that. I remember thinking that in someone's interest, the open and shut case was soon to be locked away. Someone wanted the investigation brief, Vasha's death swiftly forgotten.

Monday

I got up early next morning, and cleaned the white dust off my car. I was glad to be doing something. I wished I could as readily have cleared away the memory of the previous evening. I had lain awake for most of the night. Delayed shock, sadness for Vasha, dismay at her role in all this as well as a cowardly fear for my own safety, had kept my nerves twanging and my senses hyper-alert. I had heard and trembled at every creak of the old cottage, every rattle of the window frame, every distant car and every helicopter engine. The helicopters had come over in droves, drawn out by the moonlight and the clearer sky.

Routine exercise? Or was the search intensifying? Who was hot and who was cold? And which side was who on?

When I finally got to sleep, I dreamed I was back in Minack again. I was crouched in that space behind the wings, my ear pressed against the granite. Amplified by the rock, I heard those rhythmic footsteps. Then the footsteps turned into the ticking of the device. Louder and louder, faster and faster. Till my own heartbeat woke me. And it was just what the police sergeant and Mrs Luxford would call one of my bad dreams again.

Mrs Luxford remarked that I looked very pale but that it wasn't to be wondered at, as we drove into St Edzell's and the court room.

It was a fine fresh afternoon. A blue sky momentarily clear of wind-driven clouds arched above us. The tide was out. The grey-green rollers of last evening had become a choppy white-capped blue. The sun lit up the crescent of yellow sand. It was sprinkled with multi-coloured windbreaks and deck-chairs like hundreds and thousands on marzipan.

'Not much of a holiday it's been for you, Livvy.'

I said I had enjoyed seeing her, and that had been really the object of the exercise.

We stopped again at the traffic lights. A lot had gone on since the last time. I felt a hundred times older and sadder.

'Maybe,' Mrs Luxford rearranged her veil as we turned left, 'it'd be best if you went back to London. Come down here again in the spring.'

'I wouldn't think of it. I couldn't bear to go now.' I was surprised at my own vehemence. 'Besides, I wouldn't want to leave you.'

'Oh, I'm all right. I'll get a friend to stay.' We were almost up to the police station and the court room. I decelerated. 'Once *this* nasty old business is over – ' she jerked her head towards the entrance – 'there'll be nothing to keep you. You could go then.'

'I shall stay for the funeral,' I said.

There was a parking area just round the corner from the court room. I turned left and reversed into a vacant place. Mrs Luxford didn't answer me and I thought she had abandoned the argument. I switched off, put on the hand-brake, and opened the door for her.

As I joined her on the pavement, she said in a matter-of-fact voice, 'But there isn't going to be a funeral for you to stay for. Leastways not herealong.' She lowered her voice. 'Soon as this is over, she'll be flown back to this auntie of hers. Then maybe they'll have a funeral for her there. Back where she belongs.'

The Inquest was brief, formal and scripted. We should all

have been in that granite theatre at Minack, instead of here in the rows of Victorian benches, amongst the brown paint and the stuffy vestry smell. We were all coming in on our proper cues, saying our pieces, miming a play whose final act was therefore already written.

I heard my own voice talking. But it was as if I had divided into actress and audience and the real me was somewhere invisible in the court-room audience, watching a girl give evidence, answer questions, quietly and stony-faced.

The coroner was elderly, with thin white baby hair over a pink pate. Eyes a sad and faded blue. He was dwarfed beneath the tasselled canopy and gilded sovereign's shield. His voice was quiet, helpful, suggesting the right answer. A thin wrinkled smile when it came. A perfect prompter.

At the back of the court in the public part sat the bit players waiting off stage. William Hardaker in sober costume – dark-suited, with a white collar and a black tie. He'd had his hair cut too. He sat with his head lowered and his hands hanging loosely between his knees. They looked very red and clean as if he'd scrubbed them with all the perfumes of Arabia. His expression was ashamed. In the row in front was one of Vasha's customers, the lady in the purple velvet hat. The gentleman who'd been warming his hands at the bar fire sat next to her.

Then, well to one side, all the better to see you, frowning in concentration, Jim Curtis kept his eyes on me. Dead centre, Archie Wragg sucked the trailing ends of his moustache, not missing a word, greasy mac folded over the back of the seat. Then the newspaper roundsman, unfamiliar without his fawn overall and canvas sack. Closest to me as I stood in the witness stand, Bryan Wayne, not looking at me directly but fixing his gaze on a point in the panelling above my head.

'So you tore off the bag, Miss Browning?'

So far the actress playing Miss Browning had answered crisply and with certainty. Now she hesitated. The scene came back again in hideous clarity. The green quilt sliding away in slow motion. Vasha's ankles, the tumbled black nightdress, the neck that ended in the plastic bag. Something in that scene was very slightly out of true.

'Miss Browning, the bag?' The coroner leaned forward. 'You tore it off?'

'Yes.'

'You didn't untie it?'

'No. There wasn't time.'

'Quite. And when you did, she appeared to be dead?'

'Yes.'

'So you went for help?'

'Yes.'

'You didn't telephone?'

'I didn't think to.'

'And when you sought help, you found Mr Trelawnay, the newspaper roundsman?'

'Yes.'

'Where was he?'

'About two-thirds of the way down the lane.'

'How long did it take you to get there?'

'I'm not sure. Two minutes. Maybe three.'

'And you left the door open behind you?'

'Yes.'

'Then you went inside with Mr Trelawnay and he took over from you?'

'Yes.'

On and on. Nothing wrong with that scene. Everything above board as it ought to be. Then, 'Thank you, Miss Browning, you may step down.'

I walked past the two reporters, and sat back in my place beside Mrs Luxford. Now both our questionings were over. She patted my hand, applauding my performance.

Tall dusty windows sifted in the sunlight, sending down a static spotlight. The police surgeon walked across it to stand where I had stood. He had a brief-case today instead of a black bag. He unzipped it, took out photos, reports, handed them up to the coroner. He answered the coroner's questions immediately and without prompting, in a dull bored monotone as if he did this every day of his life. Which I suppose he did.

Cause of death – suffocation. He explained briefly how the plastic bag glues itself to the mouth and nostrils, the comparative speed and the certainty of death.

Next best way to drowning. Did he say that? Or did I think it? The dead diver and now Vasha. Both found by me. Both *inconveniently* found by me. Both bodies conveniently spirited away. Before . . . ? Before what?

The coroner was asking the police surgeon now about Vasha's physical state. In good health, good physique, well nourished. Not *virgo intacta*. Not surprising. I glanced at Mrs Luxford. She wasn't listening. A veil had dropped over her mind, like the veil she would soon drop over her face. Her eyes were fixed on the lion and unicorn in the sovereign's shield above the coroner's head as if wondering if they would ever make a move.

Now Vasha's mental state. Volatile depressive. How could the police surgeon possibly know that? Possibly hyperthyroid type. Given to sudden changes of mood. Not psychotic, no, but neurotic. Would tend to allow one small problem to weigh on her mind.

Was Vasha really like that, I wondered? Hadn't I glimpsed a different, tougher person? A Joseph's coat-of-many-colours girl? Maybe the best actress of them all?

I glanced around at the other actors. Like Mrs Luxford, Curtis wasn't troubling himself to listen to the police surgeon. He looked somehow as if he knew it all already. His eyes were still on me. Did he guess I had been in the theatre last night? Did he think I might still have the letter on me? Would he try to get it? The cottage was empty. Might he get someone up there to search again? And what, if anything, had that letter to do with Vasha's death, and the mysterious undercurrents all around us?

I slid my gaze sideways to Bryan. He gave me a wan smile and raised his brows. He pointed outside, mimed that we should meet in the side street afterwards.

I nodded, held up my car keys to indicate I was parked there.

Car keys. Door keys. Nothing had so far been mentioned about the key that Vasha had lent to William. Was it important? Obviously not. Vasha had taken her own life. Alone.

The police surgeon was being dismissed, the sergeant summoned. They passed each other on their way to the stand. The sergeant glanced meaningly at the clock. They smiled at each other. Soon over. A matter for congratulation.

Once again, we had evidence quickly and expertly given. The deceased had encountered trouble over the work permit. It was due to expire in three weeks' time. There was a limit to these things. Unlikely to be renewed. His chest expanded in a sigh. The sun winked on his chain, on William's glossed-down hair as he took the sergeant's place on the stand.

William Hardaker gave evidence as the last person to see the deceased alive. I listened carefully. William had taken Vasha home about one-thirty. They'd had a bit of a barney earlier on, but that was nothing new. She had an excitable nature. They'd made it all up and she was right as rain. With *him*, anyway. Yes, he was very friendly with her, but the friendship was what you called platonic, because he, of course, was a married man.

'And she knew that?'

'Oh, yes.' He held up his left hand. A piece of costume jewellery. A thick-banded wedding ring on his third finger. Very new and shiny.

'Did you go inside with her when you escorted her home?'

'No. It was foggy. I saw her to the door, like. Then I went back to the digs. Got in about two. My landlady made me a cupper.'

'Was the deceased worried about anything?'

'That permit, yes. I must say, that really did get up her nose. Well, she didn't want to go back. Stands to reason. Didn't know what she was going to go to, did she?'

After William, the witness stand remained empty. So that was the final act. Worry about the work permit. I watched the reporters scribbling their shorthand. The policewoman leaned down and smoothed her black tights. The coroner bowed his head over his notes. Above him, the sunlight glimmered on the tasselled canopy, the gilded lion and unicorn, as it had done last night on Minack's cliffs.

Had the delivery of the letter to Minack meant Vasha was a spy? That her activities had been discovered? Had it therefore been a warning? To Curtis? Was that why she committed suicide?

The coroner was pronouncing the curtain line, 'Suicide while the balance of her mind was disturbed.'

He stood up. We all got to our feet with him. A subdued rustling sigh of tension released sounded like muted applause. There was a corporate feeling of relief, a gathering together of bags and gloves and coats. Mrs Luxford dabbed her eyes, put down the old-fashioned veil, reached up awkwardly to secure it with her hat pin.

I put out my hand to help her. Then I froze. I took the big pearl pin from her. I pulled the net to the back of her hat. The little veil made tucks.

'Too tight, me dear,' she said.

But I still stood clutching the handful of net.

Specks of dust danced in the beam of sunlight as they had done yesterday. The scene came back in awful clarity. Just before my nails ripped desperately through the bag, those faint striae in the plastic like the folds in Mrs Luxford's veil.

Where the bag had been pulled back and up, sharply from behind.

'Who could blame her?' Bryan whispered.

'For what?' My thoughts, suspicions, imaginings had swept my mind so far beyond the Inquest verdict that for a second I didn't know what Bryan meant. I felt isolated from everyone by my knowledge. Chilled. Mesmerized like a hen pheasant up a tree with the fox below.

Who would want to murder Vasha? What possible motive could there be?

Bryan saw my distress and grasped my hand. 'Given her problems, the life she led, which of us might not have . . .'

He took Mrs Luxford's arm with his free hand, walked between us towards the promenade. The autumn sun shone straight in our eyes. Mine seemed to overflow like melting icicles.

'Don't take it badly, *please*, either of you. It's a terrible shock. And an awful tragedy. But under the circumstances of her life, inevitable, unavoidable.'

'Nothing's unavoidable, if we do what's right. *I'm* not

blameless. I deafed my ears and blinded my eyes to wrong things. Sorry for her, I was . . .' I smelled eau-de-cologne as Mrs Luxford dabbed her eyes.

She was clearly upset. But even so, she would not be persuaded to come home with me. She would go to the clinic as usual. Her little mothers would expect her. She must soldier on. Do her duty. It was only a step round the corner. Bryan and I watched her pull her hat more firmly on her head, and her squat figure disappear.

'There'll always be an England,' Bryan said, and smiled.

'She's not as tough as she makes out.'

'But then neither are you. And if you think I'm going to let you go back home to an empty house . . .'

He tucked my hand into his coat pocket and began gently propelling me down the High Street towards the promenade.

'What you need to do now, Olivia, is unwind. Cry if you feel like it. Talk it out of your system.'

I was too stunned at the moment to talk or weep. But he went on talking and for that I was grateful. I saw things as in a dream. The cement slabs of the promenade, the wind whipping up the tide pools into catspaws, two children shivering behind a red and white striped shelter, the glint of the pale sun on the railings. I floated as in a dream. Stilted up on some high hysterical plane. A balloon floating untethered above an unreachable ground. Needing a firm sensible hand to earth and tether me.

'. . . been trying to put two and two together. I've even talked to the lads. Nothing tangible. Except of course that lump of scrap Brad dredged up. He said he showed it you. The Navy search is still on. We've seen them. Quite a thrill for the boys. Tell me, would you know if the diver's compressed air cylinders were empty?'

All the time, I was aware of Bryan's voice, a quiet sensible background to our footsteps along the promenade. We passed a newspaper kiosk. Still a few *Western Morning Mails*. Soon the *Evening Gazette* would be stacked up. The Inquest would be reported. The words that were said, no doubt would be faithfully recorded. And no one reading them would understand that this wasn't the truth. That the Inquest was a charade. Except me.

Me and one other.

But was the Inquest a charade? Or was it my imaginings again? Was I more in a dream than I knew? There were, after all, strong motives for suicide. Vasha was a temperamental girl. Dramatic. All those in the court, including Bryan, appeared to think the case watertight – except me.

But I had been given that mysterious errand. I had been to Minack. I – and Curtis.

What was in the envelope anyway? Would the contents throw any light on Vasha's death?

'Did you hear that heavy noise like thunder early this morning? Depth charges, my lads tell me. Trying to detonate the thing . . .'

I was suddenly aware of Bryan's eyes peering down at me anxiously. I heard his voice saying, 'That's the ninth question I've asked you, Olivia. And I'll swear you haven't heard one of them.'

I stood still looking up at him.

'As I said, Olivia, much better to talk about things like Scorpio. Be a relief for you. Keep your mind off poor Vasha.'

'Bryan,' I remember even my voice came slowly like a voice in a dream. 'It's no use telling me to keep my mind off Vasha by talking about Scorpio.'

'Why not, my sweet?'

'Because they're connected.'

His brows drew together. 'I honestly don't follow you here. Many things are tied up with it. But Vasha, no. Her suicide was for emotional reasons.'

'But it wasn't suicide.'

'What was it then, my sweet?' An arm now round my shoulders.

'Murder.'

'Darling!'

'Listen.' Carefully I explained to him about the stria marks in the plastic of the bag, and the way they showed it was pulled up and back from behind.

'But the police would have investigated that.'

'How could they? We'd pulled it apart. Besides, those marks disappear when you tug the other way. They were there one second. Gone the next.'

'So *could* you have imagined them?'

'No.'

'And that's all your evidence for murder.' He walked me on still with his arm round my shoulders. 'You can't go round saying it on just that.'

'I shall tell the police.'

'Darling.' Bryan clearly thought he was dealing with an hysterical woman. Spot the lady – Livvy, Olivia, Ophelia. I think he really had begun to worry about my sanity. A cavalcade of expressions crossed his face. He hugged me tightly as we walked towards the car.

'Do you really think they'll believe you *this time*? On *that*?'

'No,' I said.

'Nor do I.'

'But *this time* I've something else.' I told him about the errand to Minack, the envelope back in its hiding-place in the bathroom, still unopened.

'I'll take it to the police. Straight away. I'm justified now in taking it, I'm sure.'

For the whole of the length of the promenade we kept silent. Then Bryan said, slowly and gravely. 'Yes, Olivia. I think you are.'

'There's bound to be something in it, which'll *prove* . . .'

'What?'

'That Vasha was murdered.'

Bryan opened the car door for me, but said nothing.

I put my key in the ignition. It was I who said, 'But what if there isn't? That would make it worse, wouldn't it?'

'There's only one way to make sure.'

'Open it myself?'

'Of course.'

'Should I?'

'You must.' He got in the car beside me. 'And I'm coming with you.'

He talked all the way out of St Edzell's. I think he was apprehensive of what we were going to find. He tried to make light of it but I could feel his tension running underneath. 'It would be rather awful if you took the police a love letter. Or something trivial like theatre tickets . . . Worse still if it was a letter bomb you detonated on them. You'd have difficulty talking yourself out of *that*. They'd be sure you were a nut case. You'd end up locked away.'

I drove fast and I didn't answer. We turned off the highway and on to the sandy lane.

'But frankly what worries me most about your theory is something else. If Vasha was murdered, might not the same person have a go at you?'

'Why?'

The only word I spoke all that journey. The only word

that seemed to echo in my mind. The single clapper of a continually tolling bell.

'Because apparently you know even more than she did, Olivia.'

I stopped outside the cottage and pulled on the handbrake. I got out before Bryan had time to open the door. I pushed open the gate, put the key in the lock.

I went straight upstairs with Bryan following.

'That Yale lock,' Bryan said behind me. 'Anyone might take a cast and have a key cut.'

'William already has one.'

'So all those locks and bolts mean nothing.'

I opened the bathroom door. 'Could it have been William? A *crime passionel*?'

'Possibly.' Bryan shrugged his shoulders. 'But honestly, Olivia, we haven't established yet that it's a crime.'

'We shall.'

I insisted that first we fill the washbasin with water. I'd read somewhere that people did that in the spate last year of letter bombs. And though Bryan said scientifically it was useless, he did as I asked him, just to please me.

He watched me extract the envelope from behind the medicine cupboard. He held out his hand. He insisted he be allowed to open it.

'Be careful.'

'Of course.' First he put the package to his ear. Then he gently shook it. He put a small pocket magnet over it. He held it up to the lighted electric bulb. Finally with infinite care, he began to unseal the envelope.

I watched his expression as he peered into the envelope. A frown of concentration deepened into puzzlement. He put his two fingers down inside the envelope and extracted something white.

I don't exactly know what I expected. A letter containing something. Maybe a confession. Maybe a suicide note. Maybe a love token. Certainly not what was drawn out between Bryan's thin brown fingers.

My crumpled handkerchief.

Bryan held it in his right hand, while with his left he gripped the envelope, examining the inside.

'Well, that's all.' He gave a rather rueful smile. 'Something of an anticlimax.'

'But what would Vasha want with my handkerchief?'

'That's what we shall have to try to discover.' He put the handkerchief back into the envelope, and tucked it away carefully into his jacket pocket.

He went slowly downstairs. In the hall he gave me a quick kiss. 'Stay inside now. Lock all the doors. I'm going to have a long think about this. Meantime don't let anyone in.'

I opened the door. The sun had set. I could see the headlamps of cars along the highway. A helicopter flew low along the bay with its lights lit. It moved across the sky like a huge Star of Bethlehem. Flew so low over the cottage that its slipstream sent the sand particles rattling tinnily against the side of the car.

Bryan watched it fascinated, as if he saw it for the first time. He seemed suddenly to slough off his doubts. He smiled as he waved goodbye. I remember thinking that he'd convinced himself as I had done that I was sane, and I was right.

As he closed the gate behind him: 'Don't forget, Olivia. Don't let anyone in.'

'I won't, I promise.'

I didn't shut the door till he got to the end of the lane. I felt nervous. I was suddenly aware of the gathering darkness. Of the isolation of the cottage. Its emptiness. My vulnerability. I turned and walked through the sitting-room. I opened the door to the kitchen.

And there he was.

'Hope I didn't startle you, miss.'

Mr Wragg got up from the shadows, all smarminess and smiles. He had made himself quietly at home. His mackintosh was folded and draped over the back of one of the chairs. The *Western Morning Mail* was spread out on the kitchen table in front of him. At his elbow, an empty ashtray, a teapot, two cups and saucers. But no cheroot lit, no kettle boiling, no tea made. Nothing to betray his presence.

I switched on the strip light and said, 'How did you get in?'

He blinked his eyes.

'Oh, Mrs Luxford lets me have her key now and then, if there's anything to pick up. Hymn sheets, flower rotas, lists of speakers. Such like.'

'And is there?' I walked over and switched on the electric kettle. I picked up the teapot. It gave me something to do. My hands were still trembling. I don't know who I'd expected the shadowy figure to be. Curtis perhaps. My murderer maybe.

'Not today, no, miss.'

'Well then?'

'She knew I wanted a quiet little word.'

'Who with?'

'With you, miss.' Casual and comfortable, he waved his hand at the cups and saucers. 'Off the cuff.'

The kettle began to whistle. 'Over a fresh pot of tea. That would be nice.'

'How did you get here? I didn't see a car.'

'I came by bike. They're handier.'

'Quieter,' I said, meaning sneakier.

'And you get a better view of the countryside. You should try it, miss. You'd be surprised what you see from a bike.'

I set the now full teapot on the table and pulled on Mrs Luxford's cosy.

'What did you want to have the quiet little word off the cuff about, Mr Wragg?' I'd still not forgiven him for giving me such a fright.

'Not just like that, miss. A proper little chat.' He waved me to sit down opposite. 'About this sad business.' He shook his foxy head.

'What about it?'

He pushed the teapot slightly towards me. 'You going to be mother, miss? I must say I'm dying for a cuppa.'

The little blue eyes carefully watched me pour. My hand trembled. Damn it.

'You're upset, miss. And very proper too. Only natural under the circs. Seems such a nasty way to go. But believe me, miss, it's almost instantaneous. Breathe in sharpish. Plastic's warm and sticks. Can't breathe out again. But then you know all that, I'm sure. Teaching my gran to suck eggs, I shouldn't wonder. Police tell me it's getting very popular.' He helped himself to three lumps of sugar. 'For suicide.' He stirred his tea slowly. 'And for murder.'

The eyes now rested steadily on my face.

'Very female way of doing it, wouldn't you say, miss?'

'I don't really know.'

'Doesn't it appeal to you?'

'I haven't really thought about it.'

'Clean and neat. No blood. Cheap and convenient. No gun licence needed. No poisons book, that's a point, isn't it, to sign.' He shoved his chair back, turned and looked carefully all round the kitchen. 'So common it's impossible to trace. How many plastic bags are there just by us, here and now, miss?'

'I've no idea.'

'And I don't suppose Mrs L would notice if there was the odd one missing.'

I shrugged and drank some tea. I warmed my hands on the cup.

'You've known her a long time, haven't you?'

'Yes.'

'Had a real face lift here, hasn't she? Real *Ideal Home!* Must have cost a bomb, wouldn't you say?'

I nodded again.

'Ever make you wonder where she gets the money?'

'From Vasha, I think.'

'*Really*, miss?'

'Her rent, I mean.'

'Made it go a nice long way. A bit frivolous, all those luxuries. Not like your friend what's-his-name?'

'Bryan Wayne.'

'That's the chap. Now he spends his money licking those young tearaways into shape. Very generous. Ever tell you why he does it?'

'Because he's kind. Concerned about them.'

'I was hoping you'd say that, miss. Wish there were more like him. Known him long?'

'Just since I came down here.'

'Got a lot in common, I expect?'

'Yes.'

'No trouble talking to each other? No nasty pauses in the conversation? When he's around?'

I said nothing. But he didn't appear to expect an answer.

'A science master, eh? No doubt interested in mechanical things. You interested in mechanical things, miss?'

'No.'

'Of course not! Silly question. You're on the arts side. A Levels in History, Literature and Art, didn't you say?'

'I didn't say. But that's correct.'

'It was your father and *his* father before him who was interested in mechanical things. Out in South America now, your father. Chile, eh?'

'How did you know?'

'Gets on all right with the government too. Now that needs tact. Communist, they tell me?'

'Marxist.'

'Beg its pardon, I'm sure. You must forgive us country folk for not knowing the difference. You've had the odd trip behind the Curtain yourself, haven't you?'

'One . . . and on business.'

'Of course, miss. Ikons, isn't it? That was the same year you had your accident?'

'Yes.'

'Went into Charing Cross Hospital, didn't you?'

'Yes, but it was just a ski-ing . . .'

'We mustn't pry into what it was, miss. Medical etiquette! Vasha's aunt is a medical lady in Czechoslovakia. Did she ever tell you that?'

'No.'

'You used to chat with her, though, didn't you, miss?'

'Yes.'

'What about?'

'I'd only known her a few days.'

'Long enough to form an opinion, though?'

'Yes.'

'Sort of actressy, wouldn't you think, miss? You could see her performing at . . . shall we say the Minack theatre, couldn't you say?'

'Perhaps.'

'Did you like her, miss?'

'Very much.'

'You didn't resent her?'

'Not at all.'

'You didn't think she was taking up too much of Mrs Luxford's affection?'

'Of course not. I was glad they had each other.'

'Didn't you mind her having your room?'

'No.'

Mr Wragg smiled. 'Told her, did you, about your little escapade on the beach?'

'About the diver? I told her that, yes.'

'Interested, was she?'

'She seemed concerned.'

'But she was that sort of a girl, wasn't she? Giving out. Warm. Loved life, wouldn't you say, miss?'

I nodded.

'Not at all a girl to snuff herself out with a plastic bag.'

'There appeared to be reasons.' Now I was actually coming to the defence of the Inquest.

'Do you honestly think she was all that fond of a yobbo like William Hardaker, miss?'

'You can never tell.'

'Passionate, though. If you'll pardon the expression, miss . . . sexy.'

'What's wrong with the expression?'

'Some people wouldn't like it, miss. Mrs Luxford, now, she wouldn't like it.' He drank his tea, wiped his moustache. 'And knowing that you went to a good girls' boarding-school – ' he looked over the rim of the cup – 'I'm sure you and Mrs Luxford won't have hanky-panky. Upset you, if that sort of thing went on under this roof.'

'It would be no business of mine.'

'So that sort of thing *did* go on here, miss?' He had seen me hesitate. 'Oh, it's all right, miss. Mrs Luxford and I have had our little chat. You can say she confided in me. All I'm asking from you is . . . confirmation, like.'

I told him about bursting into Vasha's room and finding William there.

He smiled an indulgent smile. 'She was a lass, was Vasha!' Odd for a chapel circuit steward. 'Perhaps our William has hidden attractions. Apart from the fact that he used to work at Pendragon.'

'What d'you mean . . . *used* to work?'

A sad shake of the head. 'Our William has been a silly-billy. Our William has got the bullet.'

'I'm sorry about that.'

'Weep no crocodiles for him, miss. Our William had it coming. Our William would have got the bullet a long time ago, except for the fact . . .'

'Except for what fact, Mr Wragg?'

'There's an old Cornish saying . . . no, I tell a lie, it's an old *Norfolk* saying . . . set a sprat to catch a mackerel.'

'And you've caught your mackerel?'

His watery blue eyes gazed unblinkingly at me. 'I wouldn't say that, miss . . . yet. But to get back to you bursting into Vasha's room that night. You heard a noise?'

'Yes.'

'Sleepless, were you?'

'A little.'

'Often sleepless?'

'No.'

'You were awake when Vasha came in on Saturday night?'

'Yes.'

'What precisely did you hear?'

'The sound of her key.'

'*Her* key, miss? All keys sound alike.'

'Her footfall on the stairs.'

'Distinctive, is it?'

'Fairly.'

'You always seem to be awake, don't you, miss?'

I said nothing.

'Take anything for this insomnia, miss? Drugs or anything?'

'No.'

'And when you do manage to get to sleep, do you dream?'

'Yes.'

'Bad dreams?'

'Not very often.'

'Nightmares even?'

'Only since . . .'

'Do you sleepwalk, miss?'

'No.'

'How can you be so certain?'

'I never have done.'

'People can do strange things when they're unconscious, miss.'

'And when they're awake,' I said.

'They can become possessed. Do things they really want to, but don't allow themselves to. Specially if they found a weapon – ' he glanced round the kitchen again – 'conveniently to hand. Odd you didn't hear anything. Your room and Mrs Luxford's so convenient to Vasha's, aren't they?'

'They're close.'

'Quite.'

I was aware of his eyes fixed hypnotically on me. I stared back at him equally intently. I said, as calmly as I could, 'I don't know what you're trying to imply, Mr Wragg, but . . .'

Quickly and smoothly: 'I'm implying nothing, miss. Good heavens, no. Just a cosy natter. You make a good cuppa. I've enjoyed it. And you might just have forgotten something that a nice friendly chat could bring out. There's some that get the bullet for talking too much. And some for talking too little. Is there anything about Vasha or *any other matter* that you know but have not communicated?'

'I've told the police what I know. And they wouldn't believe me.'

'I might believe you, miss.'

'As I say, I've told everything.'

'Everything?'

'*Everything*.'

'Glad to hear it, miss.' He got up, took his coat from the back of the chair and began to put it on. 'You see, it's for your sake I'm here. No, I tell a lie . . . for everyone's sake. Do you ever tell a lie, miss?'

'I expect so.'

Sorrowfully, 'Self-confessed, dear, dear. Get a spot on your tongue for every lie, *my* mother used to say.'

'But I don't make a habit of it.'

'Like finding bodies. No, you're right, miss. That wasn't kind. Now is there anything you've got to tell me in my capacity as Security Officer of Pendragon?'

I shook my head.

'You know that anything you find out, accidentally or otherwise, affecting the security of the realm must be reported?'

'I've told everything to the police.'

'You see, miss – ' he slipped a pair of bicycle clips on to his trousers – 'you are bound under the Official Secrets Act.'

I said guiltily, 'I'm not in your Service. It doesn't apply to me.'

He straightened. 'Oh, but that's where you're wrong. It *does* apply to you, miss. To every man, woman and child in the realm. I'll give you chapter and verse. 1920 Amendment Para 1 (b).' And then he began to declaim: 'If *any* person for *any* purpose prejudicial to the safety and *interest* of the state within the meaning of the said Act *orally* or in writing . . . knowingly makes or connives at the making of any false statement or any *omission*, he or *she* shall be guilty of a misdemeanour.'

Tuesday

I was in the living-room, clearing away the breakfast things, when the Lotus drove up and parked outside. Bryan saw me through the glass and came over to the open window.

'Come for a drive?'

'When?'

'Now. I must talk to you.'

I nodded, took the last of the crockery through into the kitchen and dashed out of the front door. I was hardly in my seat when the Lotus moved off, and then took the turning over the moor.

'I thought we'd drive to Hangingstone look-out.'

'Fine.'

The Lotus screeched round the corner on to the highway, skirted the Pendragon complex, and turned left on to the winding lane over the moor.

'I'm worried,' Bryan said in explanation, but he didn't tell me why. We turned left along the half-made track to the pile of boulders at the Hangingstone look-out. When we reached the turfy hillock, he braked sharply and switched off.

'I sat up half the night thinking over what you said.'

'I'm sorry.'

'Don't be. That's the whole point. That's why I'm worried. I think you're right.'

'Murder?'

'Yes.'

'So you think I should go to the police?'

'Not yet. And this time not alone. We're going to find

out a bit more. You and I together. They're not going to be able to say you're imagining things. As they will. I'm going to see them too.' He reached over and took my hand. 'From now on we're in this together.'

It was a fine overbright morning. Somewhere high in the sky a lark sang. The air was full of moorland smells, heather and gorse, and the sun on soft marshy ground. There was the cry of sheep and the call of gulls and guillemots, and the coastline and the sea were a stage removed, a harmless glittering background.

'We've got to get some proof that Curtis can't get them to ignore.'

'You think it's Curtis?'

'Who else?'

'William?'

'Could be. Though I doubt if he's that subtle. Oh, I know he had the opportunity. But then so did you. So did Mrs Luxford. And either of you I refuse to consider. It might of course be an old flame, a customer. Or Mr Wragg might not be as old and boozy as he makes out. Security get up to some odd things. Remember the Commander Crabb case?'

I shook my head.

'Too young.' He smiled. 'Well, Crabb was a British frogman who dived under the Russian cruiser *Ordzhonikidze* berthed in Portsmouth harbour on a courtesy visit. The intention was to discover frequency details of the latest Russian sonar anti-submarine equipment, since British mines were being designed to explode on its sound-wave emissions. It was the last dive Crabb did. The Government announced that Crabb was missing after underwater trials at Stokes Bay, miles from Portsmouth. And the CID came round and tore out pages of the register at the Sallyport Hotel where Crabb had been staying. On both sides, undercover agents were working frantically. Then nearly a year later, his headless and handless body was washed up on the Sussex coast.'

Bryan paused for a moment, frowning down at the view below. The wash of a speedboat in the bay. The ships, hull down on the horizon, the flight of three helicopters no bigger than mayflies.

'In other words, when it comes to national security, the authorities can do anything. And that's why I'm worried. You're caught in the crossfire. Olivia, there's been one murder. We've got to make sure you're not next on the list.'

'How?' I asked in a still, small voice.

'Keep our mouths shut, and find out what we can. Fore-warned is fore-armed. Now I've been thinking, there are similarities between the Crabb case and Scorpio. Crabb found what he was looking for, and the discovery killed him. I think the same thing happened to your diver friend. How did a professional frogman with two compressed air cylinders manage to drown in comparatively shallow water?'

I shook my head.

'Have you ever seen a drowned man, Olivia?'

'No.'

'Had he any bruises? Marks of violence?'

'None I could see.'

'In the half light, and with the shock of it, you might have missed a lot. After all, the eyepiece was shattered. That might have been caused by the sound . . .'

'What sound?'

'That, none of us know, darling. But I think we might guess this device, this Scorpio, normally homes on some refinement of infra or ultra sound. But sound's a strange thing, Olivia. It has good and evil potentialities, particularly ultra and infra sound . . . above and below the threshold of hearing. Sound waves can be used to map or as a warning radar. They can even kill.' Bryan screwed up his eyes and rubbed his chin with his hand. 'I've been giving a great deal of thought to Scorpio since Vasha's death. Now it's bound to home on *something*, some sense. Magnetism certainly comes into it, but there must be something else far more powerful and discriminating. Submarines these days go down so deep or stay in the shadow area where sonar and anything connected with conventional radio or light waves won't work. The propellers are shielded against cavitation so pure acoustic detection isn't possible. But the Russian submarines have got to *see* . . . and as I've said, it's possible to "see" through sound waves. Now we've been told that this important drop was interfered with. The device was deviated from its target. And the Navy reckon it's homed on something else. Possibly something that makes a certain range of sound.'

'Like a newly hatched duck homing on a garden roller.'

'Exactly. And what wouldn't they – ' he jerked his head at the ships and the helicopters – 'give to find out.'

In the silence I said, 'By the way, Mr Wragg came to see me yesterday.'

'Did you tell him about the handkerchief?'

'No. Should I have done?'

'I don't *think* so. Not till we've more proof.' He reached over into the glove compartment and brought out the handkerchief. 'I haven't forgotten it. I've studied it carefully. Take a good look at it yourself again.' He handed me a pocket magnifying glass. 'With this. Well? Notice anything?'

'Yes. Tiny blue granules.'

'Of what, Olivia? Do you know?'

I put down the glass and handkerchief. 'It's fluospar, isn't it? Blue John?'

'I wasn't absolutely sure. I thought it might be. You'd know better than I would. It's found round here, isn't it?'

'In a few of the coastal tin mines. Next to the cassiterite. It's a very beautiful colour. I've used it to touch up enamel.'

Bryan interrupted. 'Is it common?'

'Not really.'

'Did those granules come off the diver's lips?'

'They must have done, yes.'

'Could he have got into any of the mines from the sea?'

'I suppose so, yes.'

'And this blue stuff is down in them?'

'Just the odd one.'

'Which?'

'Wheal Fortune.' I shut my eyes and tried to envisage the past. 'There's an underground lake. Just made of water dripping down on to the loading level. It's milky blue with the fluospar.'

'Does the sea reach it?'

'At high tide, I think so.'

'Any other mine you know of where there's this stuff? *And* the sea coming in?'

I shook my head. 'I don't think so.'

'Now, try to remember.' He leaned forward quite excited. 'Is there any machinery that could make noise? Any noise?'

I thought carefully.

'No.'

'What *is* left down there?'

'Just scraps of metal and wood. Junk, old tools, chains, pulleys, kibbles.'

'What are they?'

'Buckets.'

His disappointment was palpable. 'Oh dear, we climb one foot, fall back two. Don't we, Olivia?'

'But they're searching the wrecks, according to your boys, and the wrecks don't make any sound.'

'Bits of them might shift with the tide. You see, presumably they don't know how damaged Scorpio is.' Bryan thought for a moment. Then he asked, 'How long is it since you were down Wheal Fortune?'

'About twelve years.'

'D'you still know the way?'

'I should think so.'

'Would you be willing to go again?'

I hesitated.

'If it's important to.'

He put his hand over mine. 'I'll be with you, I'll keep you safe.'

'It's not that,' I said. 'I'm not afraid of the mine. I just wonder if we ought to go to the police first.'

'Go to them afterwards. We can't really trust them. Or their friends. Do you remember what our Prime Minister said last August? That there is a spy in every organization, in every establishment however secret. There's one at Pendragon, you can bet your life. One maybe, in the police at St Edzell's. If you go and present them with that dirty handkerchief they'll label you a nut case.' He started up the engine and began to turn the car towards home. 'We must have more evidence. Then we'll show them.'

'Then,' I said sadly, 'we'll show *him*.'

I was halfway into St Edzell's when I saw the black MG on my tail. Mrs Luxford was beside me, so Curtis would know that the cottage was empty. I watched him carefully in my mirror. I noticed him about half a mile the St Edzell's side of Pendragon, so maybe he'd been hanging round the complex, killing two birds with one stone –

a metaphor I did my best to dismiss from my mind.

He was keeping his distance. A grit lorry came behind me, and while it conveniently separated us, I trod on the accelerator. Just for a few minutes, I lost him.

Mrs Luxford kept silent. Though it wasn't her day for the clinic, she wanted to pop in with some bits she'd knitted for the ante-natals. An excuse to get me to go out. Well-intentioned, I think. She sat with the little brown paper packet on her knee. She wore her formal hat with the pearl pin and veil, and a black coat, out of indirect mourning for Vasha. I'd offered to leave the parcel at the clinic for her, but she said the outing would do her good.

It was dull now, more like November than late September. There was a mizzling rain. Autumn leaves, soggy as wet cardboard, lined the gullies. Mrs Luxford remarked that the nice bit of weather had gone, but when I came back in the spring everything would look different. The daffs would be out. Spring was the time for Cornwall. She didn't actually ask me *when* I was going, but she paused for me to volunteer that information. But I was too busy watching Curtis. He was immediately behind me as we came to the top of Beacon Hill. My brake light glowed pink on the MG's fender. I wondered if he noticed the white powder on mine. I went slowly. All the way down the hill I heard the impatient throttled back beat of his engine. I saw Mrs Luxford glance at me curiously.

'Something wrong with the car, Livvy?'

'No. But it's a slippery surface.' In more senses than one.

We continued in intermittent bursts of speed and caution along the promenade. I had my eye on the lights, and I timed them exactly right. I accelerated left on the amber. But Curtis, damn him, followed on the red. Traffic up the

High Street was a solid block of cars, lorries and buses with steamed-up windows.

'Busy, isn't it?'

'Market day, Tuesday, m'dear. Don't you try to park. Drop me at the corner of the square. It's just a step along to the clinic.'

I wound down my window, and leaned out. A hearse was holding up the traffic as it made its slow way to the church in the square.

'Something up, me dear? An accident?'

'A funeral.'

'Oh.' She looked down and I squeezed her hand as we inched along, past the turning to the White Horse. When I looked in my mirror again, the black MG had gone. Curtis had probably guessed where we were going. A dark blue van nudged my rear bumper. An unfamiliar face stared out impatiently through the fan of clear glass swept by the windscreen wipers.

We turned into the square. The traffic flowed freer. The hearse had arrived at the church opposite the clinic. The mourners' cars had not yet caught up with it. But the bell had begun to toll.

I left the stream of traffic and drew into the side. I let her out about fifty yards from the clinic. Before I pulled out again, I noticed she averted her eyes from the small coffin which bore a single spray of white chrysanthemums. It looked very lonely I remember thinking. No wonder the association was painful for her.

I did an orbit of the square, to get back into the High Street again. I wanted to be on my own. Walk by the sea, if I could be sure that no one was following me.

I parked the Triumph in a large public car park streets behind the promenade. Being market day it was full, but I managed to squeeze in between a Dormobile and a cattle-truck, so my car was almost invisible to anyone running a quick eye over the place from outside. Then I walked down a side street towards the sea.

It was a quarter to five and dark as dusk. The rain was heavier. Only a few mackintoshed figures moved along the promenade. But the shelters were full of elderly people, muffled and booted, faces turned into the wet sea wind. I glanced behind. No one followed.

The lamps were lit, the jazzy decorations dropped pools of red and blue and green like spilled water-colours on the black macadam. The sea was battleship grey and white-crested, the sky an unbroken curtain of overcast. Rain and salt spray blew in my face. I walked along, head down, thinking, trying to arrange the happenings of the last few days in my mind.

In the coldness of my room last night, I had been eerily aware of the shut door on the other side of the little landing. I had lain awake listening for the creak on the stairs, a step, the turning of a key. Did I honestly believe that Vasha was murdered? If so, what could I do about it? Was she a spy? Had she discovered too much? Or ceased to be of further use? To whom? To the agent in every organization in every establishment, however secret, in every town? Was I myself in danger, as Bryan believed? Had I unwittingly involved myself? As I appeared to be suspected by everyone, was I at risk from *both sides*? Was Bryan right, once the device was found it would unravel? Friend and foe would declare themselves. The true faces would show on the wheel.

When I had drifted off to sleep, not surprisingly my spinning thoughts had taken the shape of the wheel again, with the great magnesium white explosion of the device at the hub. I must have screamed in my sleep again, because the explosion became the electric white of the bulb above my head. The wheel stopped at Mrs Luxford, sympathetic and worried. And the reason I suppose why she suggested the trip into St Edzell's today.

I stepped over a rain pool on the promenade and thrust my hands deep into my anorak pockets. Now mixed in with the break of the waves, and the traffic noises, came the grinding mechanical music from the Fun Fair. I smelled candy floss and roasted chestnuts and frying onions. Nostalgic childhood smells, their incongruity underlining the menace in which I the adult walked.

I saw lights from the Big Dipper and the Jet Whirl lightly staining the hem of the overcast. Just behind me, a car was slowly coming up. Tyres sizzled softly in the rain. Kerb crawling. A door opened. Quick steps behind me. A hand grasped my arm. Out of nowhere, Curtis had caught up with me. I don't know how he got on my trail again. Instinct, perhaps. Or that queer rapport that comes between hunter and hunted.

'Let's go somewhere we can talk.' He jerked his head towards the black MG.

I tried to shake my arm free, but I couldn't. I didn't know what I was going to do, except *not* get into that car.

'What d'you want to talk about?' I kept on walking.

'You.'

And giving up his attempt to get me into the car, he fell into step beside me, holding me close, lover-like again.

'I didn't know you were so interested.' I put on my most foolish, flirtatious face, and after a quick, keen, disbelieving glance, Curtis said, 'Well, I am. Very.'

'I'm interested in you too,' I said.

'In the same way?'

'I rather think so.' My heart was thumping heavily against

my ribs. I was afraid Curtis would feel it. In a conversational tone, quietly he asked, 'Why did you go to Minack?'

'Why did *you*?'

I realized my mistake as soon as I'd said it. I saw him smile. He hadn't known for sure it was me. He said lightly, almost regretfully, 'You're not much good at this sort of game, are you, Livvy?'

I said nothing.

'Why didn't you leave it as you were told?'

I still said nothing.

We walked straight through a huge rain puddle. It would have meant us parting company to avoid it and Curtis wasn't having that. My tights were splashed up to the knee. I saw an old lady in a shelter eye us mistily. Lovers blissfully unconscious of the rain and the discomfort of the wet.

'Will you give it to me now?' He held his free hand out to me.

'No.'

'Why not? It's my property.'

'On the contrary,' I said smartly, 'it's mine.'

Another mistake. Narrowed eyes.

'You opened it?'

I said nothing. I walked head down. My feet were wet. Curtis's fingers bit into my arm. I pushed back a strand of damp hair from my forehead. Curtis caught my hand as it descended with his free one. 'Did you show it to anyone?' He imprisoned that, too, in a lover-like clasp. But his fingers slid over my wrist, rested on my pulse. His face registered its soaring rate.

'Will you tell me who? Mrs Luxford? No?' A pause. 'Your do-good friend, what's his name? Ah!' He dropped my hand. 'Will you show it to me?'

'Why should I?'

'Because if you don't, I promise you – ' he bent his head; I felt his breath on my ear – 'I'll *make* you.'

I pretended to ponder a decision. Though my mind was as incapable of cogent thought as my heart was of beating calmly. 'All right,' I said. 'If you let go my arm, and answer me one thing.'

He immediately dropped his hands, put them both in his trouser pockets. I think he felt he was able to snatch me up at any time.

We were coming up to a shelter, this side of the promenade from the entrance to the Fun Fair.

'That all right?'

I nodded.

'Well, then, what's the question?'

I waited till we were at the corner of the shelter. Then I said, 'Why did you have to murder Vasha?' And as he stared at me, mask down, thunderstruck, I darted past the corner of the shelter, almost under a skidding taxi, across the road, and into the press of people in the Fun Fair.

A grey tide of mackintoshed figures closed over me. I pushed, elbowed, trod my way through it, keeping my head down, my eyes and ears alert. Once, way over to the left, I heard Curtis shout, 'Livvy! Come here!'

I just thrust through the crowd in the opposite direction, always keeping into the thickest press. And when I found myself outside the Ghost Train, I paid for double time round and went in.

I sat in the wooden car rocketing around on the narrow rails, twins of the skip rails sliding down into the darkness of Wheal Fortune. While we looped back and round on our tracks, I slipped off my anorak and reversed it to the black side. I pulled the hood forward over my face. Not much of a disguise, but the best I could do.

The iron wheels struck sparks. Wet string cobwebs trailed my skin. Painted ghostly faces infinitely more reassuring than the ones on my Sicilian wheel snapped at the touch of an electric switch into grey goblin illumination. Behind me and in front, children whooped with terror. I huddled and cowered in my brief haven. But fanciful thoughts gabbled inside me. My future seemed as dark and contradictory as the silly little cars rocketing backwards and forwards over the way they had come. Nothing seemed clear. Nothing had any pattern. Except that to get that device a number of people were prepared to kill.

Now Curtis knew I'd been at Minack, that I'd got whatever was in the envelope. Why had I behaved so stupidly? Why had I not simply kept my mouth shut altogether? Why on earth had I mentioned Vasha and murder to him?

I suppose in the shock of the moment I hadn't thought beyond knocking him off his guard enough to get away. But what had I expected his reaction to be? Horror, disbelief, indignation?

Mechanical maniacal laughter provided sound effects to the confusion of my thoughts. Didn't it mean that till now I'd really hoped that Curtis was *not* Vasha's murderer? That by some wave of a wand, black would turn white? The wheel would turn so fast that all the colours of the spectrum, red of blood, all would merge to make lily white? But why?

Because suddenly I knew, if murderer there had to be, I wanted it to be someone else.

I emerged from the second time round into what was left of daylight. I moved towards the entrance. I thought I saw a dark head bobbing above the crowd ahead of me, and I doubled back. I made myself smaller inside my black anorak. I attached myself to a family, stayed with them behind a screen of bobbing balloons till they went to the children's roundabout. I paused by the rifle range. A man chatting up the blonde behind the counter turned.

'Hello, Ollie.'

'William!'

'Just seen a bloke looking for you.'

'Did you say you hadn't seen me?'

William lifted the rifle, took aim carefully, fired. One of the little metal figures fell back dead.

'No. I *didn't.*'

'Why not?'

'Because I cannot tell a lie,' William said. 'Saw you go into the Ghost Train. Didn't know you was that childish, Ollie.'

'Did you tell him?'

William reloaded the rifle, raised it, closed one eye. 'I told him . . .'

'*What?*'

I put a hand on his arm. He mis-fired. The pellet shattered one of the plaster of paris prizes. Blondie clicked her tongue.

'Now look what you bin and made me do! I told him if you want to know, Miss Nosey Parker, that I saw you go out of 'ere, and pick up a taxi and go Ay Way.'

I felt ashamed. More ashamed than William would ever know.

'Thanks,' I said. 'But why?'

William fired two pellets quickly as the two targets fell and then put down his rifle. 'I'll have another lot in a minute, Blondie.'

'No reason. Just felt like it! Bloody-minded, that's me.' He took a packet of cigarettes from his pocket and shook a couple out. 'Have a pull. You look as if you could do with one.' He threw another over to Blondie.

I drew on the smoke gratefully. 'Did you know they've

given me the bullet, Ollie? They 'ave. Straight up! What's more, they won't 'ave it that it's the bullet. They call it summat else. That's what gets up *my* nose. I'll be offered a job, they say. But not yet. And not in *this* place.'

I sympathized. Then, 'Did he go? Curtis?'

'Yep. He went. Watch out he don't come back!'

He scooped up the pellets Blondie handed him, and dropped one into the chamber. Aimed and fired. William's expression was malevolent.

'I know too much, Ollie.'

'Maybe you've talked too much?'

William laughed. It sounded like the gramophone record in the Ghost Train. 'Nothing like what I'll talk now. Though I'm out of all that flap.'

'Haven't they found the thing yet?'

'Not them. It's my bet they won't either. Like looking for a needle in a haystack. It's delicate, Ollie. Touchy as a woman.'

William downed two more targets with his rifle, before lowering his voice to a whisper. For effect, not because he cared who heard him.

'Them trawlers out there dropped something that killed the target tracking signal. They'll get the device itself before they've finished.'

'How?'

'Because they'd almost got their little red mitts on it before. They're nearer getting it than we are, Ollie.'

'How would you know, William?'

'Because we driver lads know everything.' He threw another five-pence piece on the counter, with a gesture as if we were on some Texan outpost. 'Have to. We gotta know where and when to pick up from the recovery boats. We gotta know where to deliver the goods. Me Dad used to say in the war that the M/T boys knew the target before the Wingco Ops did. And the weight of the eggs.'

'Then tell me this,' I said, in for a penny, in for a pound, 'did you know, William, that Vasha was murdered?'

And I saw on his face all the expressions of astonishment, disbelief and outrage, that secretly I had hoped to see on Curtis's.

He loaded the rifle, banged its three shells away, and put the gun back on the counter.

'You're nuts, Ollie,' he said. 'Just like they say you are.'

And walked away.

I stood for a moment by the rifle range, uncertain what to do next. Blondie was not best pleased with me for scaring off her best customer. She asked me if I wanted a go and when I shook my head she indicated that I should make way for them that did.

I was now at the far end of the Fair Ground. There were a lot of people, a lot of heads and a lot of eyes between me and the entrance. The night was falling and there were black pools of shadow by the tents. But every stall had now lit powerful lamps of acid white incandescence. There was a spotlight at the top of the carousel that whirled in time to the roundabout, fingering the wet crowd's faces like prison-camp floodlights.

I walked over ten yards or so of marshy ground to the fortune-teller's tent. Only a pencil of light leaked out from here, and an orange glow from the illuminated zodiac. I flitted across the pencil of light. I crossed a no-man's-land of empty mud. I was pushing my way into the crowd by the Dodgems, when a hand grasped my arm.

I froze in my tracks. I shook my arm automatically, and miraculously the hand fell away.

A whiny voice said, 'Sorry, lady. We thought it were

someone else.' And then I turned. 'Oh, it *is* you then, miss. We wasn't sure.'

The Brothers Karamazov.

'Hope you don't mind us coming up like this.'

'Oh, no. Certainly not! I'm jolly glad to see you. Sorry I didn't realize it was you. But to tell you the truth, there's been a character following me. I thought it was him again.'

The elder Karamazov said romantically, 'Maybe he fancied you, miss.' Brad and Bill howled him down. 'Pick-pocket more likely. After something, miss.'

'I think you're right.'

'Like us to stay with you?'

'That would be nice.'

I said if they would just see me as far as the entrance, then I could walk back quickly to where I'd parked my car.

Their faces fell. Their expressions jerked me back as no amount of reasoning could have done to the sane everyday world. Three kids at a Fair had met up with an adult whom they'd once done a good turn to. They didn't expect to be asked to escort her to the exit and say goodbye again.

'After we've all been on some of the things. My treat, of course.'

I hushed down their expressions of jubilation, lest their stamping and shouting attract attention to me. I swept the boys along as if I couldn't wait to begin.

'Where d'you want to start then, miss?'

I picked the carousel, so that I was under the spotlight, perched high up astride a Victorian wooden horse, watching it flick on random faces in the crowd. Once, I swear I saw Curtis. Not far away the foxy gentleman talking to someone like William. But maybe it was a trick of the circling, whirling light.

After the carousel, the boys were hungry, and the two

younger queued at a hamburger stand, with me and Rob keeping a weather eye out for the pickpocket.

'If we see a copper shall we tell him, miss?'

I shook my head. 'Don't trust them either,' I said. Which they accepted as perfectly natural.

Hamburgers produced thirst. We had a couple of Cokes each. We hid our faces effectively behind candy floss and Red Indian balloons. We rolled pennies down the slope. Rob knocked down a coconut. They wanted a go at the rifle range. We returned to Blondie's counter. She handed out the rifles, took my money, made some crude remark about baby-snatching. I didn't mind the remark but I did mind that she remembered me so clearly.

I looked at my watch. Nearly six. I'd done my duty. I wanted to be gone.

'Just one more, miss.'

I hesitated. All my instincts told me not to wait. Curtis would not give up that easily. He was around somewhere. Go while the going's good.

I looked at their faces and weakened.

'All right. Only one, though. Then I must be off.'

Like all kids, they'd saved the best and most expensive for the end. The Big Wheel – about fifty feet high, slender and silver-spoked like a big brother of the whim wheels that hauled up the skips full of ore from the mines. A double cable joined the two and held the cars, open things, shaped like Victorian baby's perambulators. The four of us got into one, two each side, and pulled the safety-rod across our knees.

When the bottom-most three cars were full, the wheel did a quarter of a rotation. When three more cars were full it did another, carrying us right to the top. Now the whole of the fairground was spread out beneath us. I saw half a dozen dark heads that could be Curtis. A policeman and a policewoman, and a hundred huddled mackintoshed figures that could be Wragg. I saw cars spinning in rain spray along the promenade, the grey churn of waves, the narrowing strip of deserted shingle. Inland, the dark tower of the church in the square, headlights going up-hill flickering on the underside of the raincloud, the fat block of lights from the multiple store.

Then we began to move – fast and then faster. Round and round. Despite the height, I felt anonymous, safe up here. Too far up for people to crane their necks at us for long.

And then, suddenly, Brad clapped his hands over his ears and began to scream.

Blurred faces upturned to us, whiteness ruffling over the crowd like wind over dark water.

'Me ears. Oooh!'

Tears sprang into Brad's eyes. He wriggled behind the safety-bar, till I was afraid he would slide in his pain underneath it. I put an arm round his shoulder, held him against me.

I made hushing noises, demanding as if it were some oddity from his brothers if he suffered with his ears.

'Real bad he does.' Rob said. 'But it'll go off in a minute.'

The screams had clearly been mistaken for fright. We began to slow down, then stopped at the wooden platform, where we were helped out, and sent on our way with all possible despatch.

'What were all that in aid of then, tosh?' the operator demanded, but waved us through the exit before anyone answered.

'You come with me,' I said, 'and I'll run you home. Unless you would like me to take you to the clinic. There's a nurse there.'

But the earache seemed to be disappearing as rapidly as it had come.

'He gets these turns,' Rob said. 'School doctor says it's because of his tonal range. Hears things you and me don't hear.'

'There were this noise. Didn't none of you hear it?' Brad said. 'Ever so high. Like a whistle. Horrible!'

'But it's all right now?'

He nodded.

'Well, it's not far to the car park. What time are you to be back?'

'Mister said any time before eight.'

'Will he be there?'

They nodded. We sped down the side streets, full of shadows now, and pools of light from the street lamps. The cattle-truck and Dormobile had gone from the car park. The Triumph looked very exposed in the half emptiness.

We got in and I drove fast. I would have done anyway, just to please them. But I knew that it was vital to get quickly to Bryan. Some incoherent warning flashed at the back of my mind. Some information that I had been given, that I could not identify. I felt like people I've read about in battle, who know they've been hit but don't know by what or where. All I knew was that I must spill out the events of this afternoon to Bryan, and let him sift through them like a miner for ore.

Ore. The mine. Abruptly I slackened my foot off the accelerator. The turning wheel, producing the sound that Brad could hear but no one else. There was some machinery down a mine I had once seen turning.

Where?

Suddenly I remembered that visit down Wheal Fortune with Mr Luxford, when he took me to the one twenty-fathom level where the sea had broken through the undersea workings and had penetrated into the grotto – the one I had told Bryan about, with very blue water. I remembered Mr Luxford pointing out the big wheel, the opposite of the whim at the surface, actually turning with the power of the strong tide. Something that might produce sound, Bryan had said. Just as the Big Wheel might have produced the sound that caused Brad's earache, might it be possible for that wheel in the mine to produce the sound that attracted Scorpio?

I couldn't wait to get to the camp to tell Bryan. Impatiently I threaded through the traffic in the High Street, swung round the hill on to the motorway, and put my foot hard down.

'It's certainly a *possibility*, Olivia,' Bryan said. I think he was equally excited, but being Bryan, he took it calmly. He accepted the fact that we now had hypothetical answers to those sixty-four-thousand dollar questions *what* and *where*. Certain indications, he said, pointed to the possibility that Scorpio had been attracted into Wheal Fortune.

I was all for going to the mine straight away, not wasting a moment. But Bryan had pointed out that milling round the air shafts and adits in the darkness could be dangerous, best leave it till the moon was up. Besides, we would be gone for hours. The time to go would be when no one would suspect we were anywhere but in our beds.

In the light of the hurricane lamp, I looked at Bryan's face – absorbed, upshadowed, studying the contour map of the coast. I felt a mixture of gratitude and pain. He was prepared to do all this for me. Having made his plan, he would see it was carried out with military precision and scientific accuracy. A few days ago, I thought ruefully, I was the sort of girl whom men ply with drink for all the wrong reasons. Now I was the sort who falls for all the wrong men. Bryan would make an ideal husband for some other girl.

'Olivia . . . you return to Mrs Luxford's. She goes to bed around ten-thirty, doesn't she? Go up to your room at the same time. Then when the house is quiet, slip out and meet me at the turn into the motorway around twelve. Think you can manage that?'

I nodded. The events of the last few days had taught me to be devious, and devious I could continue to be.

That night Mrs Luxford and I had a quiet supper together. Then we watched television till the ten o'clock news. The usual wars and violence – the Middle East, Vietnam, Africa, Northern Ireland. Mrs Luxford sat drinking her Ovaltine and shaking her head. Before we went up to bed she went round the house, closing all the windows and locking and bolting all the doors.

'We've got to be careful, Livvy,' she said as she kissed me goodnight. 'The world is so full of such terrible things.'

Wednesday

Just after midnight, we met at the bend in the lane. The Lotus was parked on the grass, half hidden by bushes. The moor was dark and silent, the motorway deserted. Two miles behind us, the phosphorescent colours of Pendragon gave a pale halo to the night horizon. Beyond were the sporadic street lamps of St Edzell's – but ahead there was nothing but darkness.

Bryan was muffled in a duffel jacket. He jerked his thumb to the back to indicate a large bag. 'Sandwiches and a Thermos of coffee, compliments of the duty cook.'

I got in beside him. We started immediately.

'Anyone see you leave?'

I shook my head. 'Mrs Luxford was asleep.'

'Good!'

'Isn't it rather risky . . . going by car?'

'How d'you mean?'

'Someone might be following.'

We were racing through the darkness on the hill above St Edzell's. 'I'm making quite sure nobody is.'

We skirted Hangingstone Hill, then turned off to the left a mile from Wheal Fortune, and left the car in a beech copse. We started off along the old path to the mine. Bryan walked on fast in front, carrying the bag. I followed almost in his footsteps. Neither of us spoke. The wet wind had dropped. A canopy of stars glittered with the fresh-washed look of a rain-cleared sky. There was no human sound except the pad of our rubber-soled shoes, the brush of our trousers against the bracken and the brambles.

Now we were skirting the cliff edge, and I could hear the quiet hiss and suck of the rising tide, and the high-pitched chattering of sea birds. Amongst the heather, nocturnal creatures squeaked and scuffled, and from far away came the lovely flute call of an oyster-catcher. Behind us, the moon had risen, tinting the granite cliffs pale silver. The sea was quite calm, and I could see the white wash of a motorboat a couple of miles off the coast, which Bryan said would be the Navy still searching.

We started climbing up towards Wheal Fortune and could see the engine-house outlined against the sky, the tall chimney, the huge wheel. Moonlight shone like a tallow candle glow through the oriel-shaped windows. Then we came to rusted barbed wire, the brambles and the slag heaps – the deads. Even after all these years, nothing grew on them. Not a blade of grass, not a frond of bracken. But a lush growth grew all round the old stamping shed. Ivy, thick-stemmed as young spruces, and a line of trees along one wall, joining their high foliage like some stylized scene set. Bryan brought out his torch, shone it slowly round.

'What are they?'

'Bay trees. What the wicked flourish like.' I tried to smile. I had never been frightened of Wheal Fortune before. Its familiarity was part of my childhood. But I was frightened now.

'No such thing as wickedness. Just differing loyalties.'

Why had he said that? The words sounded odd, reflected back at me from the old walls.

He had stopped quite still as though he was listening again.

'It's – just the echo,' I said. 'The echo of your own words.'

'There are some sounds,' he said cryptically, 'that you cannot hear.'

'Then why try to listen?'

'I'm not listening. Sometimes . . . you can *feel.*'

'Ghosts . . . ?'

I could certainly feel them. Thin veils of cloud were drifting over the sky. Moonlight shone fitfully on a deserted, silent landscape. No bird calls now, no scuffling of mice. Nothing but ghosts here. Ghosts of miners and mine captains, tut workers and tributers, sump men and trammers and balmaidens. Ghosts of my father and me, listening to old Mr Luxford's stories: the day the beam broke and trapped the shift at the eighty-fathom level: the horse and cart that disappeared near the Paxton air shaft: the farmer's dog which Mr Luxford had gone and brought up from the hundred-fathom, miraculously alive after a fall down the pumping hole.

'Mind how you go! Some of the shafts were never walled.'

Bryan walked like a cat, treading softly, testing the ground before putting his weight on it. We came to the whim wheel that brought up the skips full of ore from the levels. Round a tumble of granite and mortar that had once been a wall, we walked on to the roofless engine-house, standing on the crumbling rock floor where the hundred-inch cylinder had been, looking up at the empty windows of the bob loft. Mr Luxford once told me that here used to be all painted and whitewashed, the floor scrubbed so clean that a miner could eat his 'croust' off it, curtains at the window, and even potted geraniums.

Times had changed. And changed again. What would Mr Luxford say to the search, to Pendragon, to Scorpio, and all that went on herealong now? Yet were they so different? If you looked beneath the whitewash and the potted plants to what had gone on below surface. Death and disaster again. Search. Exploitation. Greed. And before that – war, rebellion, wrecks and wreckers.

The wheel spun. But it came full circle.

'Is it here? The entrance?'

I shook my head.

'Come on then, Olivia! Let's get a move on!'

We picked our way out over the rubble. Moonlight varnished the leaves of the ivy that clung to the chimney-stack. They made a papery rustling sound in the light wind. And again Bryan paused, glanced over his shoulder.

Nothing.

A rusty iron handle, part of one of the old eggshaped kibbles, lay crumpled against a stone wall. Beyond that was the drop down the pumping shaft.

'Not here?'

'God, no!' I shivered. 'We need to be over to the left.'

I pointed to the scarcely visible grass-covered dyke, two foot wide and shallow as a grave, that ran towards the west.

Bryan shone his torch. '*That?*'

'Yes.'

With me leading this time, we walked along the rusted track. The moon threw our distorted shadows ahead – Bryan's head and shoulders superimposed on my ankles and feet. Eerie – like some cloven-hoofed creature or some monster of the deep.

We picked our way past the reedy hollows of the old waste drains, where lambreths filtered out the arsenic deposits, past the ruined sorting shed where balmaidens had stood breaking the ore with their hammers.

Then we were on the part of the track where the unstamped ore was brought up on kibbles from the working level to the sorters. A bit of old rail showed up like some buried toothroot in empty gums. The dyke was still dotted with old spillage – lumps of cassiterite, dark as lava, glittering bronze in the moonlight, the colour of a girl's dancing pumps.

The wind was freshening. It brought in the tang of the sea to mingle with the smell of old stone, marshy ground, dog daisies and moss. We followed the rail track up a gentle gradient. Ahead was a thick tangle of bracken.

I pushed my way through. Suddenly the ground dipped sharply under my feet. On either side the bracken and blackberry bushes grew thick and high, disguising the true depth of the hollow. For a second, I was afraid that the entrance would have been filled in, or buried by a fall.

'It's here somewhere. Can you shine your torch?'

Before he did so, Bryan stood on the rim of the hollow and took a long careful look round. In the clear night air, it was like being on top of a masthead. The outline of Wheal Fortune's ruined houses, the moor, the fields, showed blanched and deserted in the moonlight.

Then, apparently satisfied, Bryan jumped lightly down, and thrust his way behind me. The beam of his torch stabbed forward, then to one side, spotlighted the brick arch of the entrance – and the remains of the rusty iron track leading steeply down . . .

When the mine had shut, this entrance was sealed off with an iron door like a vertical manhole cover. Mr Luxford used to heave it back before we could get in. Now the old iron door lay inwards on the ground, rusted away, as full of holes as a skeleton.

Ease back the brambles, tread down the bracken, and the hillside opened. Aladdin's cave without the need for the magic word.

The smell was the same, though. Bending our heads under

the archway, straightening in the tunnel, it filled our nostrils and lungs like inhaling the air of a disused factory chimney. Mr Luxford used to say the sharpness in the nostrils was the rock holding the smell of the old gunpowder, and the rest was the crumbled cassiterite, stale air and the sea. The smell dilutes as you get nearer the air shafts and the adit mouths.

But I hesitated.

'Why so slow?'

Bryan pushed in the small of my back. I took three steps forward. The gradient was wickedly steep. My feet sank into the dust of powdered rock. The torch cone spread and disappeared into fathomed darkness. The glint of the rails melted with it. The walls and roof glowed darkly round us.

It was the opposite of Aladdin's cave. A long unending cavern of all shades and degrees of darkness. No visible treasures. No golden chests. No jewels. Only the modest glint of the lode and the polish made by long-dead hands on granite walls, as the men rode up 'to grass' on the old skips.

The rail gave way to steps, steeper still. Step upon step, down and down. There was an iron rail polished like the walls, cold and slippery to the touch. Loose in places. A rusted socket and nail rattled as I rested my fingers, sent thin crackling echoes into the darkness behind and in front.

'Careful, Olivia! Don't trust that rail. Try to be quiet.'

'You don't expect anyone down here, do you?'

The echo cruelly parodied the fear in my voice.

'Ssh! Of course not.'

'Why should we be quiet then? Who's to hear us?'

'Sound vibration could disturb the roof.'

Why had I come? Because I wanted to find out what was real and what was false, I answered myself. Stop the wheel.

See the true expressions on the faces. But was that *really* the reason?

The steps finished at the fifty-fathom level, a gallery stretched away from us on both sides into inky blackness. From those horizontals, other stopes led off. The rock was honeycombed with galleries and holes.

And still the drop continued. A vertical iron ladder now against the face. Bryan went first this time, cautiously testing every rung. There was a continuous clink from the bag he carried in his left hand, and the squeak of our rubber-soled shoes. The white bat of his torch flew vertically downwards, dwindling all the time like a candle slowly going out.

Somewhere in the darkness, water dripped rhythmically. The steady drip magnified and echoed, so that it sounded like an infinitely cautious footfall.

Then from down below, 'OK, Olivia! Take your time! Count the rungs. Twenty-three is loose. Careful!'

His torch came up towards me. A white ghost hand without an arm. I began the descent, counting as he had said.

'Good girl!' Bryan squeezed my arm as I stepped down to join him. There was another steep slope. The granite was running with moisture, the air warm. Then more steps, wider this time and less steep, and we had reached the hundred-and-twenty-fathom level.

The figures were still scratched clearly on the rock face. An old kibble stood on an abandoned strip of rail. The roof here was higher, supported by great vertical wooden beams. Black mouths of galleries and stopes gaped in all directions.

For a moment, I was confused. I shone my torch round. The entrance to the hundred-and-twenty was as baffling as the faces on my wheel.

'Come on, Olivia. Which?'

'This one,' I said.

Bryan dipped into his pocket and brought out a compass. 'Going south. Seawards. Sounds right.'

I walked cautiously. Every so often, branch tunnels led off to the left and right. But I didn't hesitate now. I remembered parts of this one, familiar over the years. The close timbering here, where there'd been several godsends, the strange rock formation like stalactites here on this roof above.

We walked to the side of the tunnel. What was left of the tram rails was twisted and caught at our feet. Finally, the track gave out. We were walking on the horizontal under a low roof. Timbers set aslant like flying buttresses held up the lean of the granite, emphasized the sensation of the whole place caving in. They were speckled with a bright orange fungus. The air smelled of decay. It was like being down the Roman catacombs, and I tried not to remember the thirty miners entombed in this mine.

There was a sudden eerie rattle. I'd caught the heel of my shoe in a piece of broken chain.

Bryan stopped dead. 'What was that?'

'This chain. I . . .'

'No. Something else. Further back.'

He switched off his torch. We were plunged into dimensionless darkness.

'Listen!'

'It's the sea.'

'Behind us.'

I strained my ears. 'Water dripping. I heard it further back.'

I strained my ears. Nothing else. I put my cheek to the rock face. The quiet rattle of a pebble against an iron rail, followed by a silence too absolute, like a held breath. Then the soft cautious rhythm of footsteps.

Someone was following.

'Keep very still!'

Bryan put his mouth right against my ear. I nodded. I could hear clearly now. Certainly footsteps. One person only. Probably in the stope immediately above us – the hundred-fathom level.

'Who?' I'm not sure if I said it aloud, because Bryan didn't answer. I listened, my heart hammering, thinking to myself I had set the wheel in motion. Now nothing would stop it.

'You said nobody saw you?'

'No.'

'Then you told someone?'

'Of course not.'

'You haven't discussed this possibility with anyone else?'

'No.'

'You've never mentioned the flooded level?'

I shook my head.

'There aren't any maps of these mines, are there?'

'Not that I know of.'

'So whoever it is, doesn't know exactly where to go?'

He put his finger on my lips for me to keep silent. For minutes we stayed there, glued to the rock, listening. The steps became fainter. Disappeared.

'He's going further away.' Bryan's voice sounded relieved. 'Lost himself.' He pulled at my arm. 'Now let's get a move on!'

He switched on the torch, walked forward. The tunnel widened out. We picked our way over boulders that had fallen from the roof, past a mass of broken machinery, great circles of metal with serrated edges.

'The end of the line?'

'Almost.'

'I can hear the sea.'

Not far away the funnelled thresh and sigh of inflooding water. Cooler air touched my face. From here on, the floor of the mine was littered with chains, bits of cable, kibbles, shovels and shammeling. The side where the track had been was strewn with lumps of cassiterite that had fallen off the overladen kibbles. There were ominous piles of powdered rock – godsends the miners called them because they gave warnings so often of worse to come.

Now the tunnel bent to the right. Rounding the curve of it, the sound of waves came clear and echoing.

What would we really find before the tunnel opened out? A sea-flooded mine-working? The broken machinery of the end of the hauling winch? Empty water like the empty beach? Rocks that looked like dead divers? More of Ophelia's strange imaginings?

Without shining our torches we could feel the rise of the rock roof above our heads, the opening out of the chamber.

'I can smell water. Are we here?'

Bryan's torch fingered the roof, picked out a great column of rock, twisted like an elm tree – a 'horse' of ground left as a support. And then behind, the sheen of water.

We were entering the great cathedral-like chamber of the hundred-and-twenty-fathom level. A century ago, the ore from the submarine workings was loaded and winched up from here. Over the years, the sea had reached the workings. And at high tide the wave-tops came up above the height of the floor, joining the lake tinted with Blue John to the sea outside.

I'd remembered it as breathtakingly beautiful, more beautiful than any Majorcan or Sicilian blue grotto. Now I wasn't so sure. The lake still shone its milky luminous blue in the torchlight, catching the beam, circling it with an iridescent halo. The walls sparkled with cassiterite, and white quartz and beryl. Maybe beauty is in the circumstances. I was aware now of the ugliness and pathos of the tangled metal, the abandoned skips, the remnant of the steel cable leading to the flooded working where the dark wave heads danced in.

'Where's your wheel?'

I pointed to the left. 'Over there.'

'Wait here till I have a look-see.'

He scrambled over intervening rocks on to the ledge overlooking the flooded workings. His torch flung his pointed shadow like an ink-blot over the blue water behind him. Olivia's friend. The good kind Bryan. Why Olivia would remain so touch-me-nottish. How disloyal I was, I thought to myself.

Bryan eased himself along the ledge to where the cable disappeared upwards. I watched him kneel down. His face was upshadowed in the reflected light of his torch. I knew by his expression that he had found it.

I thought of Aladdin's cave again, complete now with its modern treasure. Not the mineral sapphire of the blue pool, or the thick glittering bands of lode. But *that.* Infinitely more valuable, it seemed, than any jewel.

'Come and see!' Bryan waved me over. He smiled a wide, exultant, different smile.

He put down his bag and focused his torch beam on the silver shape fixed to the hub of the old wheel. Scorpio. No bigger, as William had said, than a nice size codling.

'So that's Scorpio,' Bryan said. 'Impressive, eh?'

'I was just thinking the opposite.'

'That's because you don't understand . . .'

'What don't I understand?'

'Its power. Its range. The damage it can do. In that tiny compass.'

'And do *you* understand?'

My tone made him glance sideways, but he didn't answer. He felt in his bag and brought out what looked like a large screwdriver.

'I thought you'd got a Thermos in that bag?'

'That's right!' He leaned over the edge of the ledge.

'Seems to me there's only tools and – '

'Damn Wilkins! Careless lad!'

I lifted out a scuba mask with a small cylinder and harness. ' – *this*.'

'Thought maybe I'd have to take a look underwater.'

'You came prepared.'

A shrug. 'Why not?'

Bryan began tapping with his screwdriver on the metal rim of the base wheel.

'You're not trying to get the thing off, are you?'

'Heavens no! That's killed one man already!'

'The diver?'

'Obviously.'

I leaned over beside him, my face near the water. Tap, tap, tap. Dit-dah-dit. Twanging seawards through the rising waves.

'What are you doing, then?'

'Vibration test.'

'Sounds like Morse code.'

'Do you know Morse?'

'No.'

'All tapping sounds like Morse to those that don't understand it.'

'But why a vibration test?'

'Safety measure. Might be explosive in there.'

He stopped tapping and straightened.

'But if there is, what's it to do with us? We need to get out now and tell someone. Before it goes up.'

'It won't go up. Not unless it's interfered with.'

'What are you worried about, then?'

'Lest, my dear Olivia, it too disappears.'

'Like the diver?'

'Exactly. That's why we have to wait.'

'For what?'

'You'll see.'

'But I don't want to wait.'

I made as if to stand up. He put a hand on my arm.

'You can't go. You've forgotten Curtis.' He jerked his head towards the way we had come.

'You *know* it's Curtis?'

'Of course.'

'How?'

'That would take too long to explain, my dear Olivia. Remember what Wragg said. Throw a sprat to catch a mackerel.' He sighed. 'Every man has his Achilles heel.'

'And Curtis's?'

'You.'

Bryan dipped into his pocket and brought out a small revolver. 'Curtis, as we know, is a Russian agent. If the worst comes to the worst, we may have to use this.'

I stood up and then shouted, 'No, that's not true! I don't believe you.'

I made a grab for the gun, and Bryan snatched his hand away. He stood up and shone his torch full on my face. He didn't try to stop me shouting, which was odd. And I remember him actually smiling and saying in a quite emotionless voice, 'You as well. That I hadn't expected. It makes it infinitely easier.'

Before I had time to ask him what he meant by that, he jumped to his feet. The sea water in the workings glowed suddenly in a swelling fan of luminous green. I put my hand up to my mouth to stifle a scream. Behind the fan of underwater light swam a black shape. Then the torch and arm broke surface first like the sword Excalibur, followed by a round black head and masked face.

My Sicilian wheel had come full circle. The dead diver had come back again.

I must have said that aloud for Bryan said, 'Not the same diver. That one was winched up by helicopter.'

Looking at Bryan's face, I remembered his expression two days ago when the helicopter had flown low and blown up the sand. He had realized *then* how my handkerchief had managed to climb up on the cliff side, but he had said nothing.

Now I remembered other things, his intense interest in all I had found, his repeated questions. Words once interpreted one way now took on a new and sinister meaning. The Sicilian wheel was turning faster and faster. Bryan's face was changing. My heart started hammering. My mouth was dry. Thoroughly scared now, I began to draw away from him.

He grabbed my arm. 'And *this* diver is going to stay alive.'

'How?' Curtis's voice came sharply from across the chamber.

'Ah, our friend at last!' Bryan pointed the gun towards the voice. 'I was beginning to think we would have to make even more noise to attract your attention. I watched you following in the rear window of the Lotus, and twice I was worried you'd lose us. I need you, Curtis, to answer the question you just asked. *How* is this diver to stay alive?'

'By keeping away from Scorpio.'

'Too simple, Curtis. Scorpio is why we are all here.' Bryan paused. 'The question is *how*, Curtis. And you will tell us *how*. The *quid pro quo*? The price of your knowledge? The girl.'

'Blackmail, Wayne, murderous blackmail! But then you are a murderer.'

'I am a soldier in a war, Curtis. Your side's words, not mine.'

'Then put that gun down. You should know – ' Curtis was walking unhurriedly towards us – 'Scorpio will go up if you fire it. As you see . . . it doesn't explode on impact. Only at a certain level of audible sound. If you fire, it'll be curtains for everyone.'

'And if I don't then you'll detach Scorpio for us?'

'Give me time to think.'

'Five seconds. We're in a hurry. My colleagues and I have a rendezvous.' The muzzle of the gun now rested on the side of my head. The hand that held it was steady. 'Counting from *now*!'

There was a moment of silence. I could hear the rush and suck of the waves, Bryan's rhythmic breathing. Then I saw him feel in his pocket with the hand that carried the torch. Something rattled and crackled.

'Three seconds gone.'

Curtis began to whistle through his teeth. People do odd incongruous things under stress. He was whistling the only tune he seemed to know. The song from the 1930's, the one he kept playing in the White Horse, the one he had whistled at Minack . . . *no more money in the bank.*

'Four seconds . . . at five, I pull the trigger!'

'Hold it!'

'You give in?'

'I parley, soldier. I have a question. How do I know you won't kill Livvy even if I do get it off for you?'

'My word.'

'Not enough. Let Livvy go and stand over there. Away from Scorpio. She'd only be in the way.'

A dreadful daunting certainty came into my head that Scorpio was going to explode anyway, and this was his way of giving me a chance to survive. Something of the same thought must have been in Bryan's mind.

He hesitated. Curtis didn't press him. He just went on whistling.

'How long to take Scorpio off safely, Curtis?'

'Thirty-five seconds, soldier.'

'Then all right, I agree.' I saw him smile. 'But I must take precautions. How do I know *you'll* keep your word? First put your hands together in front of you, Olivia.' The gun pointed. I did as I was told. A length of rope bound my wrists fast together. And then came the worst moment of all. A plastic bag descended over my head.

'A very apt precaution, don't you think, Curtis? When you come across here to show us how to work on Scorpio, she can go and stand over where you said. But she will have this over her head. Time will be short for her too. If you don't keep your word . . .'

Bryan pulled the bag over my head. As he had done with Vasha. My knees shook. I felt sick, half suffocated before it had begun.

And still Curtis whistled. That damned tune . . . *no more money in the bank*. Only now as if to turn it into a dirge, he'd stuck on the last few notes *dah-dah de de. Let's put out the lights* . . . Let's put out the lights . . . Let's put out the lights.

I almost caught my breath, drawing the fatal plastic to my

lips. I clenched my bound hands hard. *Put out the lights* . . . I'd got the message. Bryan's fingers began to pull at the plastic. The bag tightened.

'You have thirty-five seconds, Curtis . . . starting from now!'

In one lightning movement, I lunged forward at the light and crashed my two bound hands down hard on Bryan's left wrist. The torch dropped heavily on to the ledge. I kicked it towards the water. It spun, went out.

There was immediate total darkness.

I started running. I heard scuffling behind me, the sound of a fist crashing down, someone groan.

Then the diver must have come out of the water. A cone of yellow light drenched me, fixed me. And almost immediately, a spurt of hot light – a shot. The gun fired. A body alive or dead hurtled on top of me.

The echo of the shot magnified a millionfold. The darkness caught alight in a massive magnesium flare. There was a rumble like thunder, a tremendous explosion. The ledge shook and shivered. A hurricane wind knocked the breath right out of me. Choking and gasping, I felt myself being hurtled through a nightmare of falling rocks and endless blackness . . .

Alive.

I opened my eyes. Or at least I made the act of opening my eyes. For a moment, I thought I'd been blinded. Killed. Dead and buried. Then I felt the grit heavy on my lashes and in my mouth. The suffocating smell of dust and explosives in my nostrils. I was pressed down and trapped in total darkness. Metal cold as a gun dug into my forehead. A man's hand gripped my shoulder. I thought in terror: the nightmare again, but a living one. Bryan Wayne and I alone have survived.

I licked my dry lips. Bryan Wayne then still had the gun. In a moment he will kill me. He probably intended to kill us both anyway. I moved my head gingerly. The remnants of the plastic bag crackled. The grip on my shoulder didn't tighten. The weight on top of me shifted. Fingers touched my face, my neck. A voice said, 'Livvy.'

'Jim.' I raised my head. Tears washed down my cheeks. Emotion blinded and choked me. I was incapable of stringing a sentence together.

'Are you all right, Livvy?'

'I am now.' My voice quivered. A warm cheek just touched mine.

'Anything broken?' He felt for my hands. 'Come on! Stand up! Try your sea legs. OK?'

'I'm fine. What about you?'

'Fighting fit.'

'What happened?'

'I got Wayne down. But he leapt along the ledge and fired. That's when Scorpio went off. He was right on top of it.'

'So they're both . . .'

'Dead. Yes. As he intended us to be. Once they'd got Scorpio, he'd have to kill us both.'

I shivered. I felt more sick and shaken and sad than frightened. After the immediate shock and terror of it all my mind couldn't quite take in the implications of the situation. It was enough to be alive. And alive together. I suppose in the end that's what it's all really about.

'And now where the hell are we? You haven't a torch, have you?'

I shook my head, though he couldn't see me. 'Mine's smashed, blast it!' I heard him feel through his pockets, rattle a box of matches, a scrape and then the flare of a flame.

He held it aloft.

We were in a high-roofed tunnel of granite that disappeared upwards into darkness ahead. Behind us, a solid wall of boulders. Shut tight as Aladdin's cave.

Then before the light of the match died – a glint of real treasure under our feet.

'Rails,' I said. 'The old skip rails.'

Jim lit another match. 'Does that mean they lead to the surface?'

'I don't know. There are so many stopes. But they did once.'

'Come on, then!' He took my arm. 'Hold tight together. We'll make it somehow.'

I remember thinking a long time ago there are things we can hear in the voices of the people we love above and beyond the words they say. I didn't doubt that we would. But I remember adding what seemed a gloomy rider that if we didn't it would be bearable because we were hand in hand.

We walked fifty paces before lighting another match. The stope still continued upwards. We examined the roof and the walls. We counted the matches.

There were thirty-two. Every time we lit one, I thought there'll be a blank wall of rock ahead. And every time the match burned out, darkness seemed to drop like a black plastic hood, more terrifyingly than before. We kept a hand on the wall of the tunnel, the way the old miners had done, feeling it glassy smooth under our fingers. And every few paces Jim Curtis tapped on the rock with his pocket knife – *dit dah dit dah.*

'Morse?' I asked.

'Yes.'

'Bryan signalled that way through water for the diver.'

'Yes, I saw the launch in the bay. But quartz can carry sound even further. You never know. Someone might hear.'

We walked on, turning our ankles on fallen rocks and lumps of cassiterite, treading deep sometimes in dust, sliding on slippery bare wet granite.

The twenty-first match showed up a tangle of metal about fifteen yards ahead. A disused kibble on its side. Another set of rails.

'Double tracks. Could be one of the adits. One truck went down, pulling the other up.'

'Keep your fingers crossed for it,' Jim Curtis said.

'That's unlucky down here. Sign of the devil.'

'Then pray for it, girl.'

We stumbled upwards more hopefully but no faster. Still putting a cautious foot forward before resting any weight on it. My heartbeat thickening at every forty-ninth step, lest the light disclose a truly dead end.

The twenty-seventh match flame bent backwards. The phenomenon had no significance to me. My face felt cooler. But I had alternated between too many hot and cold sweats on the long walk up for it to mean anything. Jim, however, let out a shout and hugged me. The match almost fell out of his hand.

'See that, Livvy! A draught! Air!'

Ten dark paces on, I could smell it. Dog daisies and gorse and sea smell.

Then a strange mirage or my eyes were getting so used to the darkness that I could almost see. I swore I could make out Jim solidifying out of the darkness beside me.

'Light, Livvy. Look!'

Like a ragged half-risen moon above and ahead of us – a glimmer of light. There were sockets in the rock now, and even strands of rusted metal where the cable used to go.

We used them as handholds pulling ourselves up. It was like being terribly thirsty. I felt I couldn't wait for that first gulp of fresh cool air. But it wasn't that. It was as if I'd just become aware of how frightened I'd been. For the last few yards where the light came, there were tiny cushions of green moss and sea pink. It was like life itself reaching down. Now I saw in front of me a tangle of brambles and bracken meshing the adit mouth.

Jim thrust them apart. We scrambled through.

The adit had come out on to a rocky platform not far from where I found my handkerchief and met Bryan. Sound impulses then as clairvoyant as any knockers' warning had probably caused the rockfall.

We sat on the scrubby stony grass, drinking in the smell of the air and the sea and the dog daisies. We were halfway up the cliff. There was no one else in sight. There was still a long scramble either up or down, but I didn't care.

Jim put his arm round my shoulders and tilted up my face.

'The last time you kissed me,' I said, 'it was to stop me talking.'

'That's why I'm going to kiss you now. It may over the years be necessary to do it very often. You have an inordinate capacity for turning up at the wrong times and asking the right questions.'

'So the first diver was killed by the device?'

'Yes.'

'How?'

'Scorpio has a protective mechanism against being tampered with.'

'What?'

'Scorpio works by sound . . . audible and inaudible.' He kissed me. 'More than that, I can't say.'

'But you didn't know where he'd found it?'

'How could we? It was disabled. Off track. Homed on an unknown sound generator. We knew the Russians had an agent here helping the divers off the trawlers. But we didn't know who. Certain people even thought . . .'

'Me? How could they!'

'I know of certain people who even thought it was me.'

'You? How could they!'

'And so you had to be misled. To protect you. The more you knew, the more you were in danger.'

'Like poor Vasha. She was working for the British?'

'That I can't tell you. Nor who works in which department and area. Let's put it this way, her work permit would have been automatic. Her interest in William was centred on who might pump a big mouth.'

'Too long a tongue, too short a hand.'

'Not these days.'

'So she'd rumbled Bryan?'

'Probably.'

'And he knew she had?'

'Yes. Things were getting dangerous for her.'

'So that night at the White Horse . . . you passed some sort of code message?'

He nodded. 'A warning to go.'

'Too late,' I said. 'Poor brave Vasha.'

'So you see why I wanted you out of harm's way. Back in London. And *not* just out of a sense of duty.' He smiled. 'You were in danger from both sides.'

'You mean in everyone's way?'

'You knew just that bit too much.' He put his arms round me. 'Now you know just that bit more. Which is why you will certainly have to marry me.'

'Why?'

'Orders from above. Can't let you go.'

He pulled me to my feet. We looked out to sea. The Russian trawlers still kept their vigil out on the horizon. The sea was swinging in with a slight swell, glittering and glinting in the morning sun. The long stretches of sand were deserted. My Sicilian wheel was still. No faces showed on it.

And then suddenly, coming up a steep path from the beach, I caught sight of an orange tousled head. Round glasses glinted in the sun.

I leaned forward and called out, 'Brad! Hello!'

And before I'd time to ask him if his earache was better, he shouted back, 'Ow now, miss, not again! You ain't been and got yourself stuck. With him?'

' 'Fraid she has,' Jim Curtis called.

Brad clambered up beside us. I noticed he was holding his two hands in front of him. His face was solemn.

'We-ell, if you want help, I can't stop now. Too busy.' He jerked his head for me to come to one side with him. He indicated we should turn our backs on Jim Curtis. Very slowly then he opened his two hands, revealing in the middle of that delicate pink oyster shell, a rusty old hub cap.

Into my ear, he whispered, 'It. Don't you see, miss, I've found *it*.'

I watched him bound away in the direction of the camp.

'And we've found it,' I whispered. But not aloud. And I didn't mean the device.

Jim came over and took my hand. 'Better go and see what we can do about the kids. But first . . .'

As I said, it began with a kiss. It continued with one. And it ended with many.

Also available from Magnum Books

CHARLOTTE VALE ALLEN

Running Away

Isabel Gary is forty years old, beautiful, glamorous, talented – every woman's dream figure.

But Isabel is tormented . . . by the memory of the beloved husband who had died so tragically young . . . by the heartache of a rebellious teenage daughter who seems determined to destroy herself . . . by the growing demands of a lover who appears less and less ideal . . . by the mounting pressures of a challenging job that thrusts her into a TV world of sudden success and cut-throat competition . . . and by the magnetism of a man whom she fears to love lest her hopes be betrayed yet again . . .

NANCY BUCKINGHAM

The Other Cathy

Emma's first meeting with Matthew Sutcliffe on a misty moor gave her no inkling of the trouble to come. She was horrified to discover that he had been convicted of murdering her father and recently returned from fourteen years transportation in Australia, determined to clear his name.

Already Emma's life is tinged with tragedy as her cousin Cathy is dying of consumption but she finds a new life as her hostility towards Matthew changes to love. Their persistent attempts to clear his name lead to a horrifying revelation: if Matthew didn't commit the murder, then someone else in the family did!